# CURVY AND BRIGHT

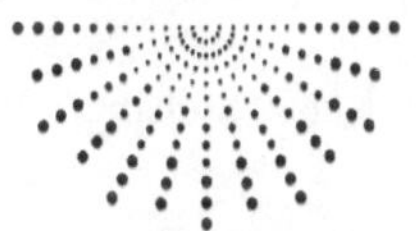

KELSIE STELTING

# CONTENTS

# SERA

"*Y*ou'll be okay without us, right?" My mom asked me as she tugged on her winter coat to leave for her shift at the hospital.

Just as I was about to answer, her pager went off. She looked at the device attached to her waistband, eyebrows knitting together. Her mind was already at work, thinking about patients and cases and calls to other doctors she needed to make.

"I'll be fine," I told her, but she was already picking up her phone, rapidly responding to some email or text. She brushed a strand of hair out of her face and leaned on the counter for support. "That's good," she mumbled, still looking at her phone.

I stared at her green scrubs, trying to remember the last time I'd seen her in regular clothes. It had been weeks, at least. She was always in a lounge set at home or scrubs at work. That was all her life consisted of these days.

With a sigh, I turned and went to sit down on the couch in our living room and turned on the TV. "Same as always," I muttered.

We lived in a beautiful house atop a hill, one of the nicest in Garland, with a view of the city twinkling in Christmas lights below. However, we hardly spent much time here. My parents were always busy with their jobs at the local hospital.

"James!" Mom called in the general area of the bedrooms. "We're going to be late."

Dad walked hurriedly into the open-concept living area, his winter coat already on over his bright-blue scrubs. "Ready," he said, running fingers over his curly hair to smooth it down. "Although you seem occupied," he commented with a small smile.

"Yeah, one sec," Mom said, still glued to her phone. "Did you see that article going around?

It's insane what they're saying about the flu this year."

But Dad was already on his way over to me. He kissed me on top of the head. "Text me if you need anything and be home by ten. You know the drill."

I nodded. "Got it, Dad."

Luckily, my parents didn't have to worry too much about me going out by myself. The small town of Garland was pretty safe. Probably the safest town in America, if I had to bet. Our crime rate was practically zero.

Probably something to do with how much everyone here was obsessed with the giving spirit of Christmas. Plus, Garlanders all knew and looked out for each other.

Mom and Dad finally made their way to the door. They pulled on their hats, and my mom called out, "Bye, Sera!"

"Be safe," Dad added as he closed the front door behind him.

I waved before turning back to the TV.

This had been our routine for a while now, ever since I was old enough be left alone without a babysitter. They would leave, and I'd watch TV and then go hang out with my friends or occupy myself at the shops in town. But tonight was different.

Tonight was special.

It was almost time for the lighting of the tree in Cider Center.

Legend had it that you could make a wish as the star on top lit up and that wish was sure to come true. People came from all over the world to make wishes of their own.

My friends would be there, and they were expecting me. We never missed it.

Meanwhile, I couldn't remember the last time my parents had gone. Maybe when I was two?

They were always working long shifts at the hospital. I knew they loved me, but healthcare was their passion, and they were good at it. The hospital and its patients counted on the Lopezes to be there, and it was hard to do your job with your child hanging around.

Which is why I was thankful I had a really great group of friends. They were the ones I could count on to be there for me no matter what.

Pushing off the couch, I went to the bathroom attached to my bedroom to get ready. I did my best to tame my curly black hair with hairspray. Then I put on some lip gloss and grabbed my coat so I could head out the door.

It was a short walk down to Cider Center and mostly downhill, which meant I found myself amongst the buzzing crowd of tourists and locals within minutes. Being surrounded by people made me feel a little less lonely.

A tall gentleman, probably about my grandfather's age, stopped me at the corner of Main and First. "Hey, you're Dr. Lopez's daughter, right?"

I stopped and smiled at him, used to the greeting. "Yeah, I am."

I had my mom's same olive-toned complexion, dark eyes, and black hair, so a lot of people recognized me as her kid when I was out and about.

The guy smiled at me, almost as if he were looking at my mom instead of me. "Your mom really helped me get over a nasty case of pneumonia in the fall. And your dad was great, too. Garland is lucky to have them."

"Thank you," I said with a rigid smile. "I'll let them know you said that. I'm sure they'll appreciate the kind words."

"Well, Merry Christmas!" He waved and walked toward Cocoa Corner, the coffee shop nearby. I waved back, even though he couldn't see me anymore, and kept making my way down to the lighting of the Christmas tree.

It wasn't a minute later that I got stopped again by someone else who wanted me to pass along their regards to my mom. They said she really helped with their son's appendicitis.

And then, one more time, someone stopped and asked me to tell my parents they said hi.

Finally, I made it to the square, wondering if I should order a ski mask on our family's online shopping account. Then maybe I could get through town without being recognized.

Mulling over the idea, I searched the crowd until I found my friends. Bethany and her bright red hair stood out first. Then Belle caught my gaze and waved at me right away. She had the kind of smile that made you feel so seen and special. I went to join them, and it wasn't long before Carolyn and Holly were there, too.

After greeting each other, we stared up at the Garland Christmas tree. It stood over thirty feet tall, covered in bright lights and beautiful ornaments. All it was missing was its star.

Everyone in town seemed excited to make a

wish, but I knew Christmas wishes didn't always come true.

When I was seven, I had wished on the star for a pet unicorn, and I definitely hadn't gotten one. The legend had to be like Santa Claus, which parents made up to make their kids behave all year.

Even so, as the mayor climbed the ladder, star in hand, I couldn't help but feel the pull to make a wish.

As he placed the star carefully on the tree and it began shining bright, I closed my eyes.

*I wish...*

I let myself whisper it.

*I wish I could be more than Dr. Lopez's daughter. I wish I could be seen for me, as Sera.*

It felt about as realistic as getting a unicorn.

2

PAXTON

*I* made it to the bottom of the snowboarding course, coming to a smooth stop in the fresh powder which reflected the harsh glow of spotlights overhead.

I could do this course in my sleep for how much I'd practiced it over the last month.

While most kids my age were enjoying winter break this time of year, I was working harder than ever. Even the word "break" was as bad as a four-letter word to my dad.

No school meant I had even more time for snowboarding practice and competitions. So I practiced around the clock while my dad coached me. Even this late in the evening when the slopes were closed to the public and everyone else was going to the Christmas tree lighting in Cider Center.

Dad came toward me, his boots crunching in the snow. A stupid part of me hoped he'd say we were done. But he motioned his hand like a cowboy with a lasso. "Again," he called. "And get a tighter grip on that second jump. You're losing points by being sloppy."

So, no Christmas tree lighting this year, either. I hadn't gone to one for years now.

My chest ached at the loss, but I ignored it, grabbed my snowboard, and made my way to the lift so I could do the course again.

See, what they didn't tell you about being a teen athlete headed for the Winter Olympics was this: it wasn't nearly as glamorous as people made it out to be.

Instead, it was hours and hours and *hours* of practice.

Every day.

Imagine doing the thing you loved so much that it practically became a full-time job with overtime and no vacation days.

That's what it was like to train for the Olympics as a snowboarder. For the most part, I liked training and competing to be the best.

But tonight? Part of me just wanted to be a regular seventeen-year-old hanging out at Cider Center and making a wish on the tree. I'd been feeling that desire more and more lately.

But as Dad liked to remind me, being the best meant showing up even when I didn't feel like it. The only person who wanted it more than me was my dad.

Snowboarding was my passion, but for him, it mattered more than anything. Sometimes I wondered if that gold medal was more important to him than me.

What would happen with us if I finally got that gold medal one day?

What would happen if I didn't?

I tried to clear my mind as I approached the top of the mountain. It did no good to have a distracted mind. Snowboarding required 100% focus. Less than 100% could mean injury or worse.

Besides, I knew my dad wanted the best for me.

That's why he had me training so much.

There were lots of competitions ahead of us, and I needed to be prepared. My next big competition was just a couple of weeks away, on

Christmas Eve. There was also a small competition leading up to it, but small or big didn't matter in my dad's eyes. They were all important. All needed to be won.

I hopped off the magic carpet lift, ready to go through the course again. I skated to the top of the run and sat down to clip my back foot in place.

When I glanced back up, I couldn't help but notice the small town of Garland down below. The entire city was lit up like something inside a snow globe.

I sat there for a moment, watching all the ant-sized people buzzing around the tree in the town center. It was like I was in a trance, just wishing for a moment that I could be a normal kid enjoying winter break. That someone could see me as more than an up-and-coming snowboarding star.

My whole life, I had dreamed of doing this. Now that I was here, snowboarding was my whole life. I just wanted something different for once. Something more.

Someone to see me for me.

As if by magic, the star at the top of tree lit up suddenly.

Now the town really did look perfect.

"Let's go!" Dad called up the mountainside at me.

So I pushed up, edging my snowboard along the slope.

And I took off.

# 3

## SERA

Since my parents couldn't come to me on their lunch breaks, I went to them. I could tell they felt guilty for how many hours they worked, and eating lunch together was their way of making up for all the time they spent at the hospital.

So the day after the tree lighting, I walked all the way across town to the hospital. It was near the highway that led out of town in case there was an emergency too big for the hospital staff to handle and specialists were needed.

By the time I made it to the cafeteria, I was sweaty under my coat and scarf and my hair was going every which way thanks to the friction from my stocking cap.

My mom stood up and picked some snowflakes from my hair. "You look like a winter fairy princess, sweetie."

I took off my coat, scarf, and mittens and sat down across from them. "More like the abominable snowman," I quipped. My stomach growled. It had been a long walk. Thankfully, my parents had already gotten my favorite: chicken strips with extra fries. Plus a side salad.

With a doctor and a nurse for parents, I was guaranteed to have at least three servings of vegetables every day, no matter how much I protested.

At least they weren't like those "almond moms" I saw online. They never complained when I added dressing to make the salad edible.

Mom dug into a big salad, her usual, while Dad had a large baked potato with all the helpings. While Mom had always had the perfect figure, that bounced right back after having me, I'd given up being a size two a long time ago.

I was destined to be a curvy size twelve, just like Mom's older sisters in Puerto Rico. Mom said I took after them way more than I resembled her. Although I didn't get to see them very often.

"So, what do you have planned for this year's winter break, honey?" Dad asked, adding some salt to his baked potato.

I put down my fork. "Not much, unfortunately." Normally, I spent the winter break with my friends, but not this year. "All of my friends are occupied, so I'll have to find something to keep me busy besides the Hallmark Channel."

"That would be good," Mom replied, taking a big bite of salad. "Get a little active instead of spending all day glued to the screen."

"Yeah," I said. Not that I minded being "glued to the screen," but it would get boring sooner or later.

Dad wiped at his mouth with a napkin. "Maybe you could do some stuff around town. Go for a sleigh ride or something."

I had already done all the tourist activities as a little kid, and it would be no fun to do it on my own. Picking up a couple of fries, I shrugged. "I'll figure something out to do."

The loud noise of silverware clattering to the ground made me jump. I turned to see a boy clearly struggling to manage a food tray with one hand. His other arm was in a cast and sling. He looked a couple years younger than me and embarrassed that he'd made a scene.

A lady that looked to be his mom rushed over then picked up the fork and grabbed the tray in one fluid motion. "Don't worry, Michael," she reassured him. "It will get easier with time."

But Michael didn't seem too reassured. "I can't even pick up a plate, and it'll be a week before we can go home. Sounds real easy."

My chest felt tight as I watched his mom pat his shoulder and help him to a table. Here I was having a pity party about my friends being busy and people in this hospital had their Christmases ruined thanks to injuries or illness. I turned back to my parents. "That's it," I whispered.

"What is it?" Dad asked.

Straightening up with my excitement, I said, "Maybe I can help families like theirs this year. Find a way to make the holidays special even though they're stuck in the hospital. I could get gift baskets together with activities to pass the time and Christmas snacks." If these families couldn't go out to experience Garland magic, then maybe I could bring some Garland magic to them.

Mom lit up. "What a wonderful idea. You know, I could send an email out this afternoon, get you a jumpstart on some donations from the rest of the doctors."

"No, that's okay," I said quickly. "I mean, thank you, Mom, but no. I want to figure this out on my own." If she helped, it would just be another way Dr. Lopez was great. I wanted to make a mark on this town because I was Sera, not because I was their daughter.

Dad smiled. "Of course you'll figure it out. You're our daughter through and through."

I smiled back, but already my head was spinning with ideas for the gift baskets. There were baked goods from Stuffers, candy from Candy Cane Co. Maybe even some flavored popcorn from It's a Wonderful Film.

The first question, though, was *how?*

All I had to my name was about twelve dollars, and that wouldn't be nearly enough. The hospital had two hundred beds for patient care. Even if they weren't all full, there had to be dozens of people like Michael staying at the hospital for the holidays instead of enjoying their vacation in Garland.

I was starting to think that maybe I would have to ask for my mom's help after all. Was I going to be able to pull this off on my own? Or would I only be able to do it as "Dr. Lopez's daughter."

4

SERA

Instead of heading home, I went to Cocoa Corner to brainstorm with a cup of their famous hot chocolate. No way was I letting my plan fail.

Something about seeing that kid struggling in the hospital had really lit something up in me. Everyone deserved a fun Christmas, even if they would be spending it in the hospital. Before leaving the hospital, I asked one of the nurses how many kids and their families would spend Christmas in the hospital. She had said about a hundred.

So many people would be stuck in those white walls while the rest of us enjoyed the holiday at home or in cozy lodging. It didn't seem fair.

There had to be something I could do to raise funds for my project. Surely, I could rally Garland around creating some holiday cheer for a group of deserving patients. People loved supporting a good cause around here. That's why the Santa's Elves charity had been around so long. But I had to get the word out to start something new.

And I needed to figure out exactly what I'd be giving out so I'd know how much money to raise.

I jotted down a few ideas, knowing I would need baskets for kids and older patients, but most of them seemed lame. Before I was even done with my hot chocolate, I realized the perfect gift basket wouldn't find me here. I needed some real-life inspiration.

Santa's Bag down the street had some of the best gifts in town. I pulled my coat and scarf back on then made my way down there.

Surely, browsing the shelves at Santa's Bag would bring some inspiration.

When I walked in, the sound of fun Christmas music filled the store. It was teeming with Garlanders and tourists alike. Christmas was less than two weeks away, which meant it was prime time for holiday shopping.

I went aisle by aisle, spotting several cute things but nothing that seemed quite right for what I had in mind. That is until I spotted several Christmas gift baskets in a corner display. I picked one up from the bottom since the handle was covered in cellophane and ribbons. There were all kinds of great items inside. From holiday-themed socks that looked as cozy as they were cute, to holiday books, coloring sets, jars of slime, comfy-looking head-phones, and more. Not to mention snacks. Lots of yummy snacks that were special to Christmastime in Garland.

"These are perfect," I said quietly to myself. And then I turned over the price tags. They ranged from $75 to $100.

My heart sank as I did the math in my head.

I would need about ten thousand dollars to get everyone a basket.

I gulped. This was starting to seem like a much bigger assignment than I had signed up for.

But I was already committed.

"Hello there. See anything you like?" The voice came from behind me.

I turned around. It was one of the college-aged employees wearing a bright-green shirt and elf hat. "Hi," I said. "Um, I am interested in placing an order for gift baskets. A large order, actually."

"Really?" she said, perking up. She pulled out a small yellow notepad and grabbed a pen from behind her false pointed ear. I noticed how her green T-shirt made her green eyes stand out.

"The thing is," I said, wringing my hands in front of me. "I kind of don't have the money yet."

"Oh." She tucked her pen back in her ear and her notepad in her back pocket. She was about to turn away, but I continued.

"I'm trying to raise some money so I can get gift baskets for the people spending Christmas at the hospital this year," I went on.

"Aww," she said, bringing her hands to her chest. "That's such a wonderful idea."

I grinned, feeling a little less embarrassed. "Thanks, but I guess I need to figure out the fundraising part next. I just wanted an idea of something nice they could get, and I thought these baskets were perfect."

She walked over. "They're pretty popular, especially with grandparents. If you put in a bulk order, we could even customize the items inside. You'd need to order soon, though."

I stared at the gift baskets, wondering how I'd possibly make this work.

"You know," the worker said. "Maybe you could set up a fundraising booth or something." She began walking toward the front of the store, and I followed her. "Every holiday season, our bulletin board features all of the big events happening in Garland. So people can see it all in one place."

We made it to the bulletin board she was talking about. It was huge and contained all sorts of flyers for things happening in Garland.

I'd never really noticed it before. "I always forget how much happens around here this time of year," I admitted.

"Tell me about it," she said. "One year, my sister and I tried to go to everything. It was crazy. But fun."

That made me smile and wish for a sister of my own. Being an only child could be lonely sometimes.

"Anyway," she went on. "What if you did a

fundraising booth at some of these events? I bet people would love to help out. Me included."

"That's a great idea," I said, feeling way better than I had just a few minutes ago. I could make a fundraising booth–in fact, I'd helped with booths for the hospital at other local events.

"I'm Sam, by the way," she said, holding out her hand.

I shook it. "Nice to meet you, Sam. I'm Sera."

She smiled back at me. Then she pointed to one of the flyers. "This snowboarding competition is happening in a couple of days. I bet you could call them up and ask if you could fundraise there. Maybe the organization would even sponsor you. It's good publicity for them, you know."

Maybe this could really happen. I grinned at Sam, saying, "You're right. That's genius."

She brushed invisible lint off her shoulder. "I'm kind of going to school for event planning."

"Clearly you have a knack for it," I said, impressed.

She took a little bow. "Thanks."

"Thank you so much for all of your help," I told her. "I'm so glad I ran into you today. I don't think I would've come up with such a good idea on my own."

Tapping her fake ears, she said, "What are Santa's elves for?" With that, she walked off to help another customer.

Already envisioning my booth, I got out my phone and started taking pictures of all the flyers. I could do the snowboarding competition first as a test run. Since it was only two days away, I needed to get to work on my booth.

Luckily, I thought I knew where I could get one.

Santa's Elves ran fundraising booths all the time. Surely, they'd partner with me for a good cause?

There was only one way to find out.

5

# PAXTON

"You nervous about tomorrow?" my friend Grant asked me as we changed with the other guys in the locker room.

Most of the competitors had been practicing on the competition run this afternoon in preparation for the event tomorrow.

"I get more nervous walking than I do on a snowboard anymore," I joked, making a few guys laugh with me. But it was half true. I spent way more time on the slopes than anywhere else.

The competition tomorrow was what we called slopestyle, which meant there would be rails and jumps to earn the most points.

I was good at them, and I'd been practicing

my butt off. Not just to win the competitions, but because it was one step closer to the Olympics. The big leagues. Something I'd been looking forward to and working toward for what felt like my whole life.

"Are you nervous?" I asked Grant. I wondered if he'd asked me because he was feeling the pressure. Lots of sponsors would be there to scout new talent—a win could mean an influx of cash, too. That was great because this sport could get expensive.

"A bit," he admitted a little sheepishly as he tugged on a long-sleeved T-shirt.

"You'll do just fine," I said, trying to reassure him while I laced up my snow boots. I'd seen him on the run, and he'd done a solid job.

I glanced around at the rest of the guys in the locker room. Erick was shrugging into his jacket. "Five bucks says that Grant is gonna get third place again," he said.

A bunch of the guys snorted.

Grant had gotten third place in the last four competitions we'd all been at. It seemed like something was going on with him mindset-wise, but I was sure he'd snap out of it sooner or later.

Grant playfully shoved Erik on the shoulder.

"Better than going nose-first into that snowbank."

The rest of us laughed, remembering Erik's legs sticking out of the snowbank at a meet last year.

Erik rolled his eyes. "Whatever. The movie theater in town is playing Die Hard tonight. We should totally go."

Grant raised his eyebrows in interest. "I could use some downtime. Pax?" He waited for me to give them an answer.

"Let me check with my dad," I said with a grin.

Die Hard was one of my favorite movies, and taking a few hours away from the slopes sounded like the best idea I'd heard in months.

Snowboarding was fun, but it was also like my job. I hadn't felt like a regular teenage guy in ages.

"Cool, I'll see you guys there," Erik said.

He gave me a wave and was off in the direction of his cabin.

"My parents are waiting on me so we can go get dinner," Grant said. "Bye."

"Sure, see you later," I said.

I made it back to where my dad was waiting

in the lodge cafeteria. The food counter was closed, but people still sat at the tables. As usual, he was busy scribbling down notes. Every day he watched me practice. And every day he had something for me to work on.

"Hey, Dad," I said, walking up to him.

"The landing on that 1440 was a little off. I'm not sure if you noticed, but the judges will," he said, hardly looking up.

"I fixed it on the landing after," I replied.

"Hm," he said, like he wasn't quite convinced. Then he packed up his notes and got up from the table. After saying goodbye to a few people in the lodge, we began walking back toward the parking lot.

Outside, it was totally dark save for one lone streetlamp over the parking lot. It flickered, giving off an orangish glow. The ski lodge was a ten-minute drive from town, so it wasn't as lit up as the rest of Garland.

Once we got in the car, I said, "Is it cool if I go to the movies with the guys later? *Die Hard* is playing."

"What time?" he asked, putting the car in gear.

"9:30," I replied.

"I don't think so," he said as he backed out of the spot.

My eyebrows knit together as I stared at him. "Why not?"

He kept his eyes on the snowy road, barely sparing me a glance. "You've got a competition tomorrow, remember?"

"So?" I said incredulously.

"So, you need your rest, Paxton."

I sighed loudly. "Dad, I'll be fine."

"We've got to be up by five so we can make it to the slopes on time."

"On time?" I questioned. "More like two hours early. Come on, Dad."

"My decision is final," he replied, and he continued walking.

Just as I opened my mouth to say something that I'd probably regret later, my phone went off.

I sank into my seat, fuming, to check my messages. It was a group text with the guys about the movie. So I fired back a message of my own.

Paxton: I'll have to miss it. See you guys tomorrow.

My throat felt tight, and I looked out the window, trying not to cry angry tears in front of my dad. Sometimes I hated that he wanted this more than me. I needed to have *something* in my life outside of snowboarding.

I just didn't know what, or how.

ALL THE GUYS were hanging out at the top of the run while we waited for our turn. It was a slopestyle run with three jumps and three rails. You started at the top and then ended at the bottom, waiting for your score from the judges.

There were several media crews there, too, with giant cameras and some booths set up for one business or another. My adrenaline was up like it always was before a big run, but I was frustrated too.

The other guys had gone to the movies last night, then met up with some girls and took rides around town in Rudolph's slay. Cocoa corner had made too many pastries, so they got free ones as they rode by. I felt like I was missing out on life, and I was sick of feeling that way.

"Up next, Paxton Smith!" The announcer called.

I pushed up from my spot on the snow and

skated over to the bench by the top of the course. The snowboarder ahead of me was almost to the end of the run, so I sat down, closed my eyes, and visualized myself doing the perfect run.

When the announcer said I was up, I took a deep, steadying breath. Then I strapped my free foot into the snowboard and hopped over to the top. From here, it was like being at the top of the world. I could see the course below me, the city of Garland further below. All the spectators were like action figures down at the bottom of the run.

But I had to block all that out and focus on the moves I'd practiced time and time again.

After a couple hops, gravity took over, pulling me and my board down the mountainside toward the first jump. This one was smaller with a rail after, and I paid extra attention to my landing like Dad coached me.

After that, I picked up speed, going for an even bigger jump. Landing this wrong could result in injury or worse, but that's why I practiced. To do this, and to do it well.

The ground flew up under me, but my board found solid ground. I let out a small, "Yes!" inside my helmet as I approached the next jump.

It went just as perfectly as the last. And when

I hit the end of the course, roaring cheers registered in my ears. That had been as close to a perfect run as I could manage.

My dad came running out onto the end of the course and wrapped me in a hug. "That's it, Pax! Way to go!"

I grinned as I hugged him back. Even if we had our differences, Dad was the reason I was as good as I was today. And I had to admit, it felt pretty good.

I unclipped my board, carrying it off the course to make way for the next competitor. Then Dad led me to the platform where media was interviewing the contestants.

I stepped in front of the sign while reporter after reporter shoved their mics in my face asking questions about the run. That is until I heard a loud crash nearby.

"What the–" I heard the reporter say, but I was already running towards the crash.

Several yards away, and I could already see what looked like a snowboarder and someone else slowly getting up from the remnants of a booth. Pieces of wood lay scattered about, along with shreds of a foam-board sign.

But what really caught my attention was the

girl nearby who was also standing up from the wreckage.

Right away, I recognized her long, wavy black hair.

And I hurried the rest of the way to her.

# 6

# SERA

I could believe what had just happened.

Not only was my dignity seriously injured, but my knee pulsed painfully, even from my spot laying on the cold, snowy ground.

I got myself up gingerly, testing how much weight I could put on my leg.

Luckily, I could stand without too much pain, but I could tell it was going to be sore and bruised up for a few days.

After brushing snow out of my face and hair, I turned my attention to the booth. Or what was left of it, at least.

The wooden table was in shambles. No way

could it be used for fundraising again. My heart clenched as it hit me that it was borrowed. I was supposed to return it in the same good condition I'd gotten it in from Santa's Elves.

It hurt a little walk to survey the full array of damage, including the sign about my project that I'd taken hours to make. It was ripped to shreds. Luckily, I hadn't been sitting directly under the table, or I would've had more to complain about than a bruised knee.

The cause of the crash was getting up now. It was some snowboarder guy who gave me a pained look before grabbing his snowboard from the ground.

It was bad enough I hadn't gotten any donations all afternoon, and now this?

Was this a sign from the universe that this project–and my Christmas wish–was doomed to fail?

The guy said a quick, "Sorry about that," and began to leave without even offering to help.

I stood there in shock, unable to say anything. Angry tears filled my eyes.

"Hey," I heard behind me. "Are you okay?"

I turned to find a guy named Paxton.

He went to my school, but I didn't talk to him much. I knew he was the snowboarder type and that he won a lot of competitions, but that was about it.

And right now, I wanted *nothing* to do with snowboarders.

"I'm fine," I managed, starting to pick up the pieces of wood around me. I had no idea how to use a hammer, much less put something like this back together.

I was starting to wish I'd just let this be another Christmas like every other year. The kind where I stayed home and watched movies and moped around eating sugar cookies. At least then my dignity would be intact instead of in pieces like the booth around me.

"Are you sure?" he said, and I realized he hadn't left.

"Yeah," I said, probably more aggressively than I should have. But I also didn't particularly care.

A few kids nearby were laughing, my blood coming even closer to a boil.

I glanced in their direction, seeing they were a few years younger than me. Middle schoolers, maybe. "Who runs a lemonade stand in the middle of winter?" I heard one of the kids say.

Not far from them, a young reporter in a hat and scarf talked into the camera about the crash.

*So I was going to be the joke of the day in the daily news. Amazing. I couldn't believe my luck.*

"Let's talk to the young lady now," I heard the reporter say as she approached me.

*You've got to be kidding me.* I wanted to scream.

Couldn't they let me hide under a rock? Or better yet, go home and never emerge again?

"Can you tell us what happened here?" the reporter said, shoving her microphone in my face.

As if on cue, another reporter also ran up to me with their camera crew.

I stood there, frozen, with two microphones in my face, and with no idea what to say. I wasn't sure if I trusted myself to say anything.

Paxton cleared his throat, "Actually, it's our project." He walked up right next to me, still carrying his board.

The reporters turned to him, moving their microphones closer to him so they could hear what he had to say.

I gawked at him, waiting for his explanation.

He turned to me, a smile on his face. "Tell them all about our booth, Sera."

Debating whether or not I should set the record straight, I stared at him for a second or two longer. Then, slowly, I turned back to the cameras. "Actually, it's a fundraiser. Or it was before it got destroyed. There are people spending Christmas at the hospital, and I wanted to make sure it was a special holiday for them."

The reporters went on to ask Paxton why this meant so much to him, and of course, he gave the most brilliant, heartfelt answer. *So much for accomplishing something on my own now.* I just stood there in shock while he spoke, feeling like the nobody I was.

Everyone knew who Paxton was. The snow-boarding star who won competition after competition. It was only a matter of time before he won a gold medal and had his face on a cereal box. The reporters confirmed he mattered so much more than me when they signed off and began leaving without asking me anything else.

On the verge of tears, I turned back to the booth, which was still in shambles.

"Sorry to jump in there," Paxton said with a guilty smile. "Looked like you were struggling, and I'm used to talking to reporters."

My jaw clenched. "That would have been great–if you hadn't told them a big fat lie. What are we supposed to do now?"

7

PAXTON

*I* looked at Sera, surprised by her anger. "What's the deal? All press is good press, right? Well, you just got a bunch of extra eyes on your fundraiser. You're welcome."

"This is supposed to be my thing," she said with her jaw tight. "Not *our* project. *My* project. Now people will donate because it's you, not because they actually care."

"Does it matter?"

Her dark eyes bore into mine.

"I'm sorry," I said, lifting my hands. "Like I said, I was just trying to help."

"Well, I didn't ask for your help," she replied quickly. "Besides, I hardly know you. Now we're supposed to be doing this project together?"

Her comment stung a little. The truth was, I'd always had a bit of a crush on Sera. We didn't share many of the same classes because she was one grade level below me, but I'd seen her in the cafeteria and hallways at school over the years. There had always been something about her that caught my attention, even if I'd never had the courage, or the time, to go and talk to her.

"It's a really cool project," I said, hoping to make things better. I hated the thought of never having a chance with her because of this.

She looked at me with distrust. Like she didn't believe me.

"It can still be your project," I said. "I didn't mean to take it from you. But maybe I can do something to help."

She seemed taken aback at that. "Why would you want to help? Aren't you kind of busy with"– she indicated toward the course and its specta- tors–"all of this?"

"It's all I'm busy with, honestly," I muttered.

"Huh?" she asked.

"It's just… it would be nice if I was able to do something other than snowboarding. Something normal for once."

Sera huffed. "You'd probably be good at this, too."

Then, I realized what she was saying. She felt invisible. A problem I sometimes wished I could have.

"Look," I told her. "This is still going to be your project, I promise. Just think of me as your assistant or something. Put me to use. Tell me what to do. If I can help you reach your goal of helping those kids, then that can only be a good thing, right?"

"Of course it's a good thing." She sighed, biting her bottom lip. "It'll be me and my parents all over again," she mumbled.

"What do you mean?" I asked, wondering what she was upset about. Before I could ask, though, my dad came over to us. "What's this I hear about you doing some charity project, Paxton?" he demanded. "When did we talk about this?"

Sera looked between us, and my ears turned hot. "Dad, it's okay. I'll explain later."

"I can't allow you to participate in this, you know that. Snowboarding has to come first," he said.

"And second and third, apparently," I quipped,

annoyed that he was telling me all this, especially in front of Sera.

At least she had the decency to look a little embarrassed for me.

"Look, Dad, it'll be good for my image or whatever, alright? Besides, it's too late to back out now," I told him. "It's all over the news."

Dad thought about that. If there was anything he appreciated more than me giving it my all out on the snow, it was me getting known. Good publicity was important and hard to come by for someone barely up and coming like me.

His lips thinned with his defeat. "Fine, but it can't interfere with your practice times."

"But I practice more often than I don't," I argued.

"Then she can come with you for your free ride." He shrugged. "Otherwise, it's off."

Half my day was spent with me going down the trails on my snowboard without rails or jumps. The more familiar I was with my board and the snow the better.

Dad turned to Sera. "You can snowboard, can't you?"

Sera opened her mouth to answer, a little spark of fear in her pretty brown eyes. "I–"

I interjected, "Of course she can. I've seen her on the slopes. She's great."

She glared at me again, but I quickly looked away from her to keep my eyes on Dad.

"Okay, then," he said reluctantly. "Then maybe this can work." His tone said he most certainly thought it wouldn't work, but he didn't want to argue more in public than we already had.

The sound of the announcers came loudly through the speakers nearby. "The scores are in, and it's time to announce the winners!"

"Paxton, let's go," Dad said, already looking in the direction where the medals would be handed out. I nodded, going to follow him.

But Sera grabbed my hand, quickly whispering, "I can't snowboard!"

I liked how close she was to me but unfortunately, it was time for me to go. "Let me worry about that."

8

SERA

woke up the next morning, and immediately, the events from the previous day played in my mind.

What was worse—and as if everything hadn't been horrifying enough—I'd come home to find a hot cocoa stain on the tip of my nose. It had to have been there the entire time I was speaking with Paxton—and while I was featured on the local news.

I pulled my pillow over my head like that could somehow smother the humiliation.

Talk about any teenage girl's worst nightmare.

When I came home after picking up the pieces of the ruined booth, I turned on the TV, hoping to watch a comfort show. The first thing I saw? The local news report showing my interview.

Now I had an embarrassing clip of me stuttering through a response–with hot cocoa on my nose–and it would exist *forever*. At first, I hoped it was just a blip on the local news. But when I checked station's website, the video was posted for the public to view and had hundreds of comments below it.

Probably because of Paxton's appearance. Of course, he'd looked incredibly handsome on camera and spoke like a natural. Meanwhile, I'd resembled a toddler who needed a bib and didn't have a vocabulary of more than twenty words.

If that video got circulated around Garland High, I'd never live it down.

Even though I wanted to stay in bed and pretend I didn't exist, I made myself get up and get ready. I was supposed to meet Paxton at the ski lodge soon, and I still had no idea what we were going to do with this predicament. His dad said we needed to work together while snowboarding, but I had no idea how. Ice skating for fun with my friends was as athletic as I got.

Between my dreadful appearance on the

news, my lack of snowboarding abilities, and the fail of my fundraising booth, I wasn't feeling very hopeful. My Venmo account sat at fifty dollars, thanks to a text I sent out to my friends. That wouldn't even pay for a gift basket.

But I couldn't focus on that. I once asked my parents how they saw such horrific accidents in the emergency room and managed to keep working. They said they focused on what they *could* do instead of what they couldn't. That is what I needed to do now.

With that in mind, I got started by getting ready for the day. I braided my curly hair in pigtail braids like I'd seen snowboarders do, then bundled up in what I hoped would be appropriate for snowboarding. (Thanks, Google.) Then I drove to the ski slopes, stopping for a sweetened iced coffee at a little drive-through in town because I was *not* used to being up this early.

As I got closer, I admired the cute, log-cabin looking building. It was a big square with a few smaller stands around it touting ski and snowboard rentals, snacks, and lessons for all ages.

I parked in the crowded, snow-crusted lot and got out, walking toward the front entrance. That's when I noticed Paxton was near the front, leaning up against a solid log support and waiting for me. He gave me a wave and easy smile before jogging over to me so we could walk side by side. "You made it," he said, like he was genuinely happy I was here.

It caught me off guard. Surely an Olympic hopeful had better things to do than hang out with a failed philanthropist.

As we walked together, I realized just how tall he was—nearly a foot taller than me. I hadn't realized that detail before since I'd been so busy chewing him out.

That reminded me of why I was here in the first place. "So what are we going to do, and how is this going to help me with my fundraising project?"

"Cutting straight to the chase, huh?" he said as we walked towards a kiosk that said TICKET CENTER. "Well, I figured we could get you started with lessons and brainstorm our next steps."

I was a little skeptical. "Aren't you kind of busy with all this?" I asked, gesturing at the mountain where skiers and snowboarders were already shredding down the slopes despite the early hour.

He shrugged. "Kind of, but I think it's kind of cool what you're doing. I'd like to help if you'll let me."

My stomach fluttered at the compliment–especially coming from someone like him. "Thank you," I said in a small voice. "I guess we can give it a try." Even though I was getting more nervous by the minute that this would be a failure. I didn't have a lot of time to raise the money and a snowboarding side quest didn't scream *good idea.*

As we approached the ticket desk, one of the ladies pulled out a snowboarding outfit from under the large registration desk. It was lime green and came with what looked like all the stuff you needed to snowboard, including a helmet. "What's all this?" I told him.

He took the stuff from the lady and turned to me. "For you," he said. "You'll need it."

I took the outfit. "I already have warm clothes."

"Learning to snowboard is hard," he told me. "You have a water-resistant coat on, but you'll want waterproof. Otherwise, you'll be soaked by the end of the day." Without waiting for me to argue, he asked, "Is it the right size?"

I flipped the tag over, impressed that it was. "Yeah." I sent a nervous look to the slopes. "Are you really going to make me snowboard?" Now that he was handing me all this gear, it was feeling more real. Nerves made my stomach clench. Failing at this in front of Paxton would be even more embarrassing than my terrible news debut.

Paxton sent me a teasing grin, walking back toward the big lodge building. "You look like I just asked you to climb Mt. Everest or something."

"Climbing Everest seems just as likely as me snowboarding," I said, only half joking. "I don't know how to do this."

"Everyone in Garland snowboards. Or skis– but we won't talk about them."

It was supposed to be a joke, but my lips barely twitched. "Not me," I told him.

"Not even once?" he asked, seeming skeptical.

"Yeah, once, and it did not go well," I replied. "In fact, I cried so much the instructor went to get my parents half an hour into the lesson."

"How old were you?" he asked.

"Thirteen," I deadpanned.

He tried to cover the surprise on his face,

making me laugh. "I was six, but still…" I trailed off. "I hope you have a backup plan."

"We don't need a backup plan when you have me." He grinned as he held the door to the lodge open for me.

I followed him toward the ladies' room so I could change. If I was going to turn back, now would be the time. There was a waist-level window on the far side of the bathroom. Even with my lack of athletic ability, surely I could make it out. It was only a few-foot fall to the packed snow between the building and the sidewalk.

My gaze lingered longingly on the parking lot. But I turned away, going into the biggest stall to change. Paxton was waiting on me, and even though it was hard to admit, I couldn't raise this money on my own.

The outfit he'd gotten me was incredibly thick and warm. As soon as I had it on and zipped, my skin prickled with heat. Stepping out of the stall, I looked at myself in the mirror. The bright material looked amazing against my dark hair, and instead of looking like a puffy blob, it cinched in around my waist, accentuating my curves.

Feeling strangely confident for what I was about to do, I walked back out to see Paxton still holding onto my helmet and the other stuff. "Wow," he said. Then he seemed to snap out of it. "I mean, you look great. Um, ready?"

I cringed. "Listen, I'm not a pro like you. I'm not any good at this."

"Well," Paxton said, grabbing my hand. "I think it's time for that to change.

9

PAXTON

"I'm still not understanding the part where me falling on my face is going to help us raise money," Sera complained loudly as she pushed herself up to try again. "Unless you secretly have someone paying money every time I fall down. In that case, we're rich."

I stifled a smile at her commentary while watching her snowboard several feet down the slight hill we were on. Her arms waved wildly until she lost her balance and fell on her bottom again.

She had done okay with "skating," which was snowboarding with only one foot attached to the board. Now that both her feet were strapped in, she was having a harder time figuring out how to turn without getting her board wedged in the snow and flipping over.

I ran over to help her up, showing her how to flip over onto her knees while she was still on the ground so it would be a little easier.

When she was standing again, I reminded her, "You learning to snowboard will help because my dad insists on me practicing for the next competition pretty much every waking minute. This way, I get in some practice, and we also get to figure out how we're going to raise enough money to buy all those gift baskets."

Sera pulled her goggles up so they rested on the forehead part of her helmet. "I still think there could've been a better way." She gestured toward a medic sitting on a snowmobile nearby just in case he was needed. "Why can't I ride one of those things?"

I couldn't help but notice how pretty and sparkly her dark eyes were. Especially with all the light bouncing from the snow. I tried not to stare into them too long. "Employees only," I gestured toward the snowmobile. "Besides, this is good practice for me, getting back to the basics again."

"Snowboarding is life and all that, huh?" she said dryly.

"Something like that," I told her in response. We began walking back up the hill so she could try again. "I want to make it all the way to the Winter Olympics, and according to Dad, that means giving it all my time until I qualify."

"Don't you get tired of not being able to do anything else?" she asked.

"You have no idea," I muttered. But then I remembered the feeling of winning the competition yesterday. "Although, it's hard to miss other stuff when you're holding a trophy in your hands."

"Makes sense," Sera replied as we reached the top of the hill. She seemed sort of lost in thought, or maybe she just wanted a moment to catch her breath. The elevation here was a thousand feet more than Garland, and it made a difference. "Sometimes I wish I had something I was really good at. A calling, you know. My parents found theirs, and I keep hoping I'll find mine too, but no such luck."

. . .

"WHAT DO THEY DO?" I asked, realizing how much I was enjoying myself. I almost didn't want her to try again so we could just sit at the top of the hill and get to know each other better. She was easy to talk to, and it was a breath of fresh air talking about something other than my sport.

"My mom's a doctor, and my dad's a charge nurse. Both take their jobs very seriously," she said, casting her eyes down. She looked like she wanted to say more but held back.

A moment passed between us, and I could tell she was done with that line of questioning. "Ready to go again?" I said instead.

"You first," she replied. "Show me how to stop again."

I chuckled. "That is an important skill."

"I swear this is like learning how to ride a bike again, but somehow ten times harder," she added.

I grinned over at her as I turned my board so it was facing down the gentle slope for lessons. There were a couple groups around us at various levels of instruction. "Oh, come on, it's not that bad."

"Really, if it wasn't for the fundraiser, I honestly would've quit fifteen minutes ago."

I laughed. "We started thirty minutes ago!"

"And?"

Shaking my head, I said, "For the patients." With that, I snowboarded a few feet down, showing how I turned my board to be perpendicular to the slope instead of parallel. "Bend your knees and lean toward your heels to help you turn," I reminded her.

Sera gave me a thumbs-up, then pulled her goggles down.

She started down the hill, but instead of stopping by me, she kept going, faster than I thought was possible on the bunny slope. "Aaaahhh!" she screamed.

"HEELS!" I yelled after her.

Heeding my words, she bent her torso at the hips like I'd shown her and then came to a stop, wobbling for a few seconds before she fell down to her knees.

"Heck yeah!" I clapped for her. "There you go! Keep it up and you'll be ready to go on the lift in no time."

"Oh, I don't think that'll be necessary," she said, pulling her goggles up again and looking over her shoulder at me as I came to meet her. I liked how often she lifted her goggles because it let me see her pretty eyes. "It's bad enough doing this from the ground, much less having to jump off the lift first."

"I think you're being dramatic," I teased her. "You should've seen your face just now. You were having the time of your life."

She scoffed loudly but bit back a smile. "I was not."

But she unstrapped her board and led the way back to the top of the hill.

I grinned and followed after her.

This hardly qualified as practice for me, but I didn't care. Watching Sera learn how to snowboard lit up something inside of me. And it wasn't just her pretty eyes that did it or her funny commentary. I could see how much determination and grit she had trying to learn and the pride when she managed to stop just now.

It was like getting to experience the sport for the first time again, and I liked sharing that with her.

I watched Sera go down the hill again, this time coming to a much smoother stop on her own. After a few more successful tries, I snowboarded down and stopped right next to her. "I think you're ready for the lift."

10

SERA

Paxton said we should go on the longest lift which took us all the way up the mountain and then we could take the green trails back down, giving us more time to practice with less of me having to climb up and down the hill. I liked that idea until we approached the lift and I saw how fast the chairs were coming.

I stood in place like he said, my heart hammering, as the seat came up under me and took out my knees.

Scrambling, I held onto the pole between us as a bar lowered to keep us in place.

"Way to go!" Paxton said, smiling over at me like I hadn't been near a myocardial infarction.

"Thanks," I said, too breathless for a better retort.

We sat side by side on the two-person lift, a metal guard locking us in place. The snowboard dangled heavily from the one foot it was attached to, but it felt secure. Carefully, I looked down, seeing the slope about fifteen feet below us. People whizzed down the snow on skis and snowboards.

Someone on skis wiped out, and the straps of wood detached, going flying.

"Oof," I said.

Paxton replied, "See, you're not the only one who falls down."

I stuck my tongue out at him, making him laugh.

Then he said, "Let's talk about the fundraiser. I was thinking we could go directly to the businesses instead of you doing booths at events. It should be easy enough to call all of them, right?"

I nodded. I was nervous to make that many phone calls, but having Paxton helping was actually encouraging. "Should we divide and conquer?"

"I won't have as much time to call, but if you make the list, I can call over my lunch break in the middle of the day and make some calls to businesses that are open past suppertime."

"Sounds good," I said. Objectively, I was less busy than him, so it only made sense that I would do more calls.

Mulling over the list, I cautiously glanced behind us and let out a gasp. Our small town spilled out below us, looking like a toy-sized winter wonderland. I could only imagine how incredible it would look at night with all the Christmas lights shining. "I've never seen Garland like this before."

I turned toward Paxton, who I realized had been looking at me. Even in the cold, a warm flush reached my cheeks. "Do you ever get used to it?" I asked, trying to play it cool. "The view, I mean?"

He grinned, finally turning to look at Garland behind us. "I try not to take it for granted."

I looked back too, imagining this view being commonplace. The tree in Cider Center looked extra pretty with the baubles reflecting the light.

Paxton's voice interrupted my thoughts. "Remember how to get off the lift? We're close to the end."

My heartrate ratcheted up again. "Theoretically, yes," I said, my voice sounding small.

"Then theoretically, we should be fine," he replied.

If I wasn't so nervous I might have laughed. Thankfully, he reminded me what to do, "Point the toe of your board forward. Bend your knees, because it will be a little hill. If you fall, roll out of the way so you don't get run over by the people behind us."

I had to remind myself to breathe.

The closer we got to the end where the ski lift turned back around, the more the pit in my stomach grew.

"What happens if I just stay on?" I asked.

Paxton gave me a look. "You can do this, Sera."

I watched a few people in front of us get off, most of them successfully, and tried to rehearse in my mind what they were doing.

"Ready?" he asked.

I shook my head. "Not even a little."

"It's okay," he said. "I'll help keep you steady if you want."

I turned to him and nodded thankfully. "Please."

I wasn't sure what I was expecting him to do exactly, but it sure wasn't putting his hands on my hips.

My heart fluttered for entirely new reasons.

The jumping off point was coming up fast.

We were next.

Too late for regrets.

It happened fast.

"Go!" Paxton said.

I stood up from the chair, and he held onto me.

But the second my board hit the ground, it slid out from under me.

A scream left my throat as the sky changed locations, and I landed on top of Paxton, taking him down with me. When we finally came to a stop, we formed a tangled heap of limbs and boards in the snow.

Somehow, I ended up on top of him. Our noses almost touched. And even though my heart was pounding a million miles an hour, time seemed to still as he looked into my eyes. He made no move to get up or tell me to get off of him.

If we were just centimeters closer...

"Are you two okay over there?" I heard.

The spell was broken.

I got up quickly, and Paxton did the same.

I spotted the source of the question. An older man in skis had come to a stop several feet away. His blue spandex suit clung to his body like he clung to the ski poles at his side.

"You two took quite a spill," he said.

Paxton brushed some snow off his snowsuit. "We're okay."

"Thanks," I said with wave.

The guy waved back and continued skiing.

We skated the same direction and sat off to the side at the top of the run.

Now that we were shoulder to shoulder, Paxton looked at me. The expression he'd had on his face just a few seconds ago completely gone. Instead, there was a small smile on his lips. "You survived your first lift ride."

"Barely," I muttered.

He chuckled, standing up and offering a hand to help. "Come on. Let's head for the slope."

I followed him over to the top of the run, trying not to overthink what had just happened between us. It had been nothing, clearly nothing. He was probably catching his breath from me landing on top of him.

A guy like Paxton didn't like girls like me.

He was insanely good looking, talented beyond belief, and had a bright future. Me? I was *not* part of the popular crowd at all (even though my friends were the best in the world). My grades were average. I didn't have much going for me, which is why I'd come up with the fundraiser idea in the first place.

I finished strapping in my second leg and looked at the hill ahead of us. It wasn't very steep, but it was a long way to the line of trees that signaled a turn to the next descent. An image of me flailing into the tree line flashed through my mind, but I focused on the long line of orange netting that would hopefully catch me if I couldn't stop on my own.

"Are you sure you're okay?" he asked as we reached the summit.

I nodded. "Yeah, I'm fine. Sorry about earlier," I said in response. "I didn't mean to take you down with me."

He gave me a reassuring half-smile. "You've got nothing to be sorry about. It's normal to fall, especially when you're still learning. I'm just glad I caught you."

At those words, my face felt hot again, and

maybe Paxton also felt awkward because he turned his gaze back to the slope.

"So anyway," I said, trying to make the awkwardness go away. "I thought we were supposed to be talking about the fundraiser. Should we make a script or something for the phone calls?"

Paxton put his goggles back over his eyes. "Don't worry; we'll get to that. Once you've got the basics down, we'll have plenty of time to talk fundraising."

I thought about that for a second. "I'm not sure we have the time for me to get the basics down."

He laughed. "You're closer than you think."

"Close to what?" I asked. "A broken wrist? A bruised tailbone? The loss of my dignity?"

Paxton laughed then nodded toward the slopes. "Ladies first."

Even though part of me wanted to run in the opposite direction, I kind of wanted to show Paxton that I wasn't completely helpless. Besides, he looked so graceful on the board. I knew I couldn't be at his level, but I wanted that feeling of weightlessness for just a second.

So, I edged closer to the slope and let gravity do the rest.

I began gaining speed pretty quickly, and I fought the urge to scream or fall back to stop myself.

I had never attempted anything like this in my life.

And that's when my lips turned up into a wide smile. This felt like flying.

Maybe snowboarding wasn't as hard or scary as I thought it would be.

Maybe a girl like me could–

Then the toe edge of my board hit the ground, and I completely wiped out.

Paxton skidded to a stop near me. "Sera, are you okay?"

I lifted my head from the snow. "Have I mentioned this was a terrible idea?"

# 11

# PAXTON

Dad shook me awake, and I struggled to open my eyes. "Rise and shine, champ."

I groaned. "Snooze button, please," I managed.

He chuckled. "Olympians don't use the snooze button. Time to get down to the slopes." Leaving the room, he gave me some privacy to change. I let out the world's biggest sigh.

I rubbed my eyes and checked the time on my phone. It was five in the morning. The sun wasn't up yet, but I was.

Most of the time, I was used to it, but the past few days? Not so much.

With all my physical activity I usually had no

trouble falling asleep at night, but the last few nights I'd lain awake replaying my conversations with Sera. And when I wasn't replaying our conversations, I was remembering other parts of our time together.

Watching her gain confidence on her snowboard. Helping her up after a fall. Giving her pointers to improve and showing her slopes that felt as much like home as the four walls around me.

Plus, it felt good to be working toward a common goal with her–especially one that didn't involve snowboarding. It finally felt like I had something more in my life than training and competitions.

Going to the bathroom, I splashed cold water on my face and tried to focus.

It was not a good idea to get on a snowboard with your mind on other things. I had the scars to prove it.

When I walked into the kitchen fully dressed, Dad was pouring coffee into a silver coffee mug that said GARLAND, ME. He'd been using it for as long as I could remember, and the paint was all scratched. I made a mental note to get him a new one for Christmas as I grabbed an energy drink from the fridge. Coffee wasn't my thing, but I definitely needed a pick-me-up.

Dad leaned back against the counter, watching me over his mug. "You seem off lately. Distracted."

"I'm not," I lied.

I was already thinking about my plans to meet up with Sera later this afternoon, once I'd been in the weightroom and finished a cupping session. My chest did something weird every time I pictured her smile.

"Did you hear me?" Dad's voice cut through my thoughts of Sera and the slopes.

"Huh? Yeah," I replied quickly. Lies.

"I said, your next race is right around the corner," he repeated.

I nodded. "I know, Dad."

Dad didn't seem satisfied with that response. "You can't forget about what's important." By which he meant impressing potential sponsors at the competition that would give me a leg up for the Olympic trials.

I chugged down the rest of my drink.

Getting sponsors, winning meets–that was important to me. It's just that all of a sudden it felt like something else was important too.

Or someone.

Dad finally let it go, and we rode together to the gym. I had a trainer that gave me workouts that strengthened my joints for jumps and build up my core so I could keep better balance. By the time we were done, I could tell I'd be sore the following day.

With my trainer yelling commands at me, I forgot about Sera for just a moment. But thoughts of her quickly returned during my cupping session as I just laid there and the sports massage therapist applied the cups to my skin. I couldn't wait to see Sera on the slopes again.

"Are you ever not snowboarding?" she quipped as I snowboarded to base of the mountain to meet her near the ski lift like we'd planned.

"I eat and sleep from time to time."

"Speaking of," she said. She dug into her bag and pulled out what looked like a sandwich wrapped in plastic. "Here. I made extra."

I took it, and my stomach seemed to growl in response. "Thanks."

"You're not allergic to peanuts, are you?" she asked. "It's PB&J with strawberry jalapeno jelly, my favorite."

I shook my head. "Actually, it's my favorite, too."

That made her grin. "You're kidding. I've never met anyone who likes it that way."

"I found a can at Santa's Elves one time when I was Christmas shopping for Dad, and we both got hooked on the stuff."

"We probably like the same kind," she said.

Warmth went through me at the thought of Sera and I liking the same thing without knowing it. In fact, it was a little embarrassing just how happy it made me. I needed to cool it or she'd think I was lame. "Come on," I told her, going toward the lift entrance.

This lift was a gondola, which meant it was enclosed and would be easier to get on and off. Once we were inside, I sat across from her, eating my sandwich. Between bites, I said, "Let's try something new today. I think you're ready."

She looked at me with apprehension in her eyes. "What am I ready for?"

"A more challenging run," I said.

"What makes you think I'm ready?" her voice was a little higher pitched.

"It's just… you're not a complete disaster on a board anymore."

She reached across the space between us and punched me playfully on the shoulder but laughed. "I guess I have you to thank for not being a 'complete disaster' anymore. Who would've thought?"

"I told you, you just had the wrong teachers before," I said.

The gondola carried us higher and higher. Sera glanced around, probably noticing how far up the mountain we were.

"Speaking of favorites, I want to show you my favorite place," I told her. We were almost there.

The door to the gondola swung open, and workers made sure we got out safely. This time we were holding our boards so we didn't wreck into each other. She followed behind me holding on to her board.

"This is it," I told her. "Come on."

Sera followed me around a small copse of trees to a clear patch on the other side.

The sky was cloudy but covered in plenty of blue. The snow was a brilliant bright white. And below us was the rest of the mountain that faced away from Garland.

The rest of the world.

It was a magnificent view, one that I never got tired of.

Sera stood next to me. "Wow," she said, her eyes darting over the scene.

"I know," I said, thinking to myself that Sera only added to the beauty of the mountain. "It's beautiful."

We looked at the pretty view for a bit and talked about fundraising plans before Paxton said we should go to another one of his favorite spots. I was starting to realize just how big the ski area was–and how much there still was to discover around my small hometown.

To get to our next destination, we had to go down a trail labeled as blue, and my heart rate instantly ramped up because I'd only ever gone down greens. "Are you sure about this?" I asked Paxton. Blues were harder than green, and I worried I'd embarrass or even hurt myself.

But he seemed to have all the confidence in the world as he said, "You can do this."

It struck me that he was one of the few people with so much confidence in me. In fact, my mom kept suggesting she reach out to her doctor friends because she doubted that I could raise the money in time. She meant well, but I just wanted her to believe in me like Paxton did in this moment.

Feeling bolstered by his support, I started down the hill, doing a "falling leaf" pattern like Paxton taught me. It meant my board was always perpendicular to the mountain and I had less of a chance of falling on my face.

I made it down the short run without falling once, but I was so surprised by the sight of an icy building that I forgot to celebrate. "Whoa," I said. "What is this place?"

"Welcome to the ice bar," Paxton said, waving his hand in a fancy gesture before bending to unclip his board.

"How did I not know this place existed?" I asked, unclipping mine as well and following him to the rack outside the ice bar where other skis and snowboards waited for their owners.

"Probably because the only way to get here involves skis or snowboards," he teased. "It's a bit of a trek, but they've got the best hot chocolate around."

I looked at him skeptically. "I thought Cocoa Corner had the best hot chocolate."

"I mean," Paxton said, "their hot chocolate is pretty good, but the rumors say that they got their recipe from the owner of this place."

"Hm," I replied, intrigued at the idea of slope-side rumors. "Fascinating."

"Come on," he said, grabbing my hand and leading me around the side of the building. Turns out what we approached was just the back wall made from bricks of snow. On the opposite side was a bar formed entirely from ice. Glass bottles rested in an ice window at the front of the bar. There were booths forming a half-height outer wall where you could sit and drink. There were even tall standing tables made entirely of ice as well.

People gathered round with their hot drinks in hand. Several baristas buzzed around busily, pouring alcoholic drinks, mixing coffee blends, and spraying whipped cream atop steaming mugs of cocoa.

A line of skiers and snowboarders stood in

line to order their drinks, so Paxton and I fell in behind them.

"Are the menus made of ice too?" I asked him with a teasing smile.

He laughed, then added. "No menus are needed when you know hot cocoa's the best option."

"Does it come with marshmallows?" I checked.

He scoffed. "Of course. We're not animals."

That made me laugh.

I liked how easy it was to talk to Paxton. Whether we were talking about snowboarding, life, or the fundraiser, the conversation flowed. Sometimes I caught myself pretending that we were hanging out on a date, just because. But those dreams were better shoved away.

After we ordered, I asked him, "Is this the place to hang out after practice?"

He shrugged. "Sometimes. My dad and I used to come here any time I won a competition." There was a nostalgic smile on his lips, but then it faded. "But then we stopped coming as often."

Part of me wanted to press and ask more questions, but I could sense he didn't really want to talk about it. I could tell he loved his parents, just like I loved mine, but everyone had their own struggles.

Still, it was nice that he'd brought me to a place that meant so much to him. Like the mountain top.

He looked like he was about to say something, but then it was our turn to order.

"And can you add extra dark chocolate flakes, please?" he told the girl at the front. He glanced at me. "Trust me."

I did trust him, I realized. Just a few days on the slopes was all it took, seeing how kind and patient he was with me while also pushing me and having fun. Not to mention, I liked his idea of going door-to-door to the businesses in town to gather funds. He had typed out a note on his phone for me to use as a script in case I got nervous.

A few minutes after ordering, we sat on an ice bench with our hot chocolate mugs in hand. Surprisingly, it wasn't super cold while wearing all my layers.

Paxton watched me take a careful first sip. Dark chocolate flakes melted in my mouth, and I tasted what had to be the best hot chocolate I'd ever had in my life. It was sweet, but not too sweet, and had a tiny hint of sea salt and maybe caramel?

"Oh my gosh," I said, staring at the cup.

Paxton grinned and took a sip of his drink. "I knew you'd love it."

"This is like Cocoa Corner's, but somehow better," I said, taking another generous sip, even though I felt guilty for admitting it.

"Because it's the original recipe." He winked.

"Now you've spoiled Cocoa Corner for me," I joked. "I'll never want to go anywhere but here ever again."

"I guess that means a lot more snowboarding together, huh?"

The pleased way he said it had me blushing. Paxton Smith wanted to spend more time with me.

"So," I said, trying to recover from the shock, "What else do you like to do for fun? Besides snowboarding, eating, and sleeping?"

Paxton sat back, and I did the same. "Actually, I like to read sometimes. When I'm not completely wiped from practicing for some big competition, I'll stay up reading sci-fi."

"Like Lord of the Rings?" I asked, my brow knit.

"That's one of my favorite series for sure, but I don't think it classifies as sci-fi—more fantasy. I'm really liking Dune right now."

I stared at him, stunned.

"What?" he said.

I blushed a little as I said, "You do not look like the type to be a bookworm." Paxton could've passed easily for a model, and he was a certified jock… and somehow a sci-fi geek?

"Well, I'm sorry to break it to you," he said, nudging me playfully. "I'm not just brawn. I've got brains too."

That made me laugh. He laughed, too.

"What about you?" he asked. "Do you like to read?"

I shrugged. "My parents are big on grades and academics and stuff, so I study a lot. That doesn't make reading tons of fun for me."

"Did you ever want to try sports, like when you were a kid?" he asked.

I took another sip of my hot chocolate. "Maybe once when I was little, but I knew even then I wasn't very good at athletic stuff. I was always worried the other kids would make fun of me." I turned to Paxton. "Besides, my parents never pushed that kind of thing. Instead, they always made sure I had a tutor and educational TV."

Paxton grimaced a little. "All-day snowboarding practice does sound better in comparison. I'm glad you're trying sports now, though. And you're not half bad, you know."

I was a little flustered at the compliment. "I guess snowboarding has its redeeming qualities."

"I really think it comes down to having the right teacher come along," he teased. His blue eyes did that thing where it looked like they were looking deep into mine all while he wore a devilish grin.

I fought to hold his gaze while telling myself that we were just friends.

As much fun as we were having, a guy like Paxton could never fall for a girl like me. We were far too different from each other. If he caught wind of my crush, it could make him uncomfortable, and then he wouldn't help me with the fundraiser anymore. And the truth was, I needed him.

So, more than anything, I needed to keep my feelings in check and focus on raising enough money for the hospital in time for Christmas.

Snowboarding after our hot cocoa rendezvous started out well, but I faceplanted about halfway down the second trail we did. When Paxton caught up to me, he asked if I needed another break, and I quickly agreed. Snowboarding was hard work.

On the slopes, you were supposed to look out for the people in front of you. Most people gave us a wide berth, but a little kid–who couldn't have been older than five–shredded past us. His turn whipped snow in our faces as he kept going down the slopes.

Paxton cleared his goggles, and I did the same.

"Okay, I was feeling good about myself until just now," I muttered.

Paxton kept a serious face on. "Don't pay attention to that kid. He's probably had private lessons since he could walk. Besides, he'll never fully appreciate his skills because he didn't have to work at it like you."

I looked at Paxton, wondering if he meant it or if he was just being nice. He seemed sincere. "Okay," I said finally. "I guess you're right."

"I always am," he replied with a charming smile. He pushed himself up and then helped me up. "Wanna come to my place and talk fundraising? The lifts will be closing soon."

Half an hour or so later, we reached a cabin at the base of the mountain. Usually, tourists rented them out while they were in town, but Paxton held open the front door and said, "Welcome to my humble abode."

I stepped inside, curious about where he lived. "Are you sure this is okay? Me being here?"

"Yeah, it's fine. Dad won't be home for a couple more hours."

We took off our coats and ski pants, each of us down to our sweats. He ran his fingers through his hair that showed signs of his helmet.

He always had his helmet on, but now that I had a good look at his hair, I really liked it. It was long and dark blond and kind of wavy, with frosted tips. A strand was tangled in the back, and I found myself wanting to reach out and fix it, but he got it with his fingers.

"What?" he asked. "Do I have something in my hair?"

I shook my head quickly. "No."

He looked a little puzzled.

"Could I have some water?" I asked, mentally kicking myself for getting caught staring at his hair.

"Sure," he said, heading toward the small kitchen. I took a seat on their couch. It was a cozy home and looked perfectly lived in but not cluttered.

Different from my house, which usually felt big and empty when my parents were gone.

"Here," Paxton said, returning with a glass of water.

"Thanks," I said, taking it carefully.

He sat next to me on the couch, pulling one knee to his chest. "I was thinking about those care packages."

I took a sip of water and nodded before

setting the glass down on the coffee table in front of me. I tried not to think about how close he was to me.

"I remember one year when I was little, I had to spend Christmas in the hospital because my appendix decided Christmas Eve was a good time to burst." He cringed at the memory. "The nurses were nice and always tried to cheer me up. They even decorated the room for me, but it smelled like a hospital. It didn't smell like Christmas."

I nodded, intrigued.

He kept going. "I read somewhere that our sense of smell is highly tied to our memories, so if we could get a good scent for them, it might make them feel more at home."

A light bulb went off in my head. "So the smell of cookies baking in the oven—"

"Or the smell of candy canes and Christmas trees," he said, and we both glanced at the small tree in the corner of his living room.

"It's part of what makes Christmas really feel like Christmas," I said.

"Exactly," he replied. "So I was thinking… what if we made a scent part of the care packages."

I wondered how we could pull it off. "I bet Santa's Bag could make some custom air fresheners for us! Something safer than candles since it'll be in the hospital."

"They could go on the small Christmas trees in their rooms," he added excitedly.

"That's a really great idea," I told Paxton.

He smiled back at me, making butterflies erupt in my stomach. But they quickly stilled when I remembered we had to raise the money first.

I pulled out the shared list of businesses on my phone. We both crossed out the text when we had called them and entered in how much money we had raised.

"There's just a few businesses left to call," I told him. "And we're nowhere near our goal."

Paxton frowned. "Maybe it's time to start posting flyers around town."

I nodded in agreement, hoping it would be enough.

14

SERA

The next day, I showed up to snowboarding training excited to show Paxton what I had stashed away in my bag. I couldn't believe how quickly we'd become friends. I liked him, a lot, and I didn't want to think about the fact that our friendship probably wouldn't last past this project.

Pretty soon, the Christmas fundraiser would be over, and he'd be back to training for his competitions all the time—without me to slow him down.

We'd go back to school after the holidays where he'd be the tall, handsome snowboarder who could get any girl he wanted. And I'd be... me.

The girl who never fit in other than with her friend group. I'd never be noticed by a guy like Paxton.

I stared at the goggles in my hands and tried not to think about it. Why spend time stressing about painful realities that I couldn't change?

"Hey, you," Paxton said, jogging up to me. He was already in his gear—today it was a plain blue coat and black pants. "What's that you got there?"

I held up the bag I'd brought over. "Just an early Christmas gift for you," I said with a grin.

Paxton looked like a five-year-old who'd just been told Christmas had come early.

First, I pulled out the sugar cookie air freshener I'd found at Santa's bag after yesterday's snowboarding session. "I thought these would be perfect for our fundraiser. What do you think?"

He held the freshener near his nose, breathing deeply. "These smell just like the ones my mom used to make every year." He handed it back to me. "Here, before I decide to eat it."

"They have several more Christmas-themed ones back at The Nutcracker. I already let Mrs. Merriwether know we're going to need all the inventory they've got left."

He glanced at my bag. "What else ya got?"

I reached back in and pulled out a book. "Here."

He took it. "What's this?" he asked, turning over the book so he could see the front cover.

"It's a signed copy of Dune," I told him. "I found it in the used section of the bookstore. It was a lucky find."

He opened the page, staring at the author's signature. "This is amazing," he said, locking his eyes on me. "Thank you."

I felt heat radiate up my back, into my neck, and around to my cheeks. "I'm glad you like it," I stammered.

"This is the nicest thing anyone's done for me in a while," Paxton said quietly, looking back down at the book like he couldn't believe it.

"Really?" I asked, surprised. Surely a guy like him had lots of friends doing nice things for him.

He turned toward the lodge, calling over his shoulder, "We should get going."

I realized he didn't answer my question. My heart ached for him. I might not be popular, but all my friends would be bringing gifts for me to the New Year's Eve party. I already knew they'd be amazing and thoughtful, just like my friends.

We didn't talk as we stashed our items in a locker at the ski lodge and then went back outside. Despite all my progress in our lessons, I proceeded to have two left feet all afternoon, spending more time on the ground than actually standing up.

After my fifth spill, I got up from the snow, almost wondering if I should just stay there and save us both some time.

Paxton came over and helped me up.

"Thanks," I said, completely embarrassed at how bad it was. I should have been doing better by now.

"Don't mention it. Are you okay?" he asked. Even though I couldn't see his eyes behind his goggles, I could hear the worry in his voice.

I nodded, attempting to laugh it off. "Sorry for slowing you down so much today. It's like I forgot everything you taught me."

He gave me a kind smile. "It happens. You're still learning, remember?"

After a noncommittal shrug, I unstrapped my board so we could walk back to the gondola.

"Even I have my bad days," he added.

I struggled to believe that. But I hoped I could turn my bad day around. Once we reached the top of the mountain again, I took a deep breath to steady myself. Then I edged down the mountain, wanting to find the feeling of flying snowboarding could bring.

But just like last time, I lost my balance and fell.

This time, I picked myself up before Paxton could get there.

Before I could get going again, though, he stopped in front of me. "Are you okay? That looked rough."

"I'm so sorry," I said, staring off at the snow, more frustrated with myself than anything else. "I can't get the hang of it today. I just keep falling."

"Me too," I thought I heard him say. But before I could ask him and be sure, he added, "Let's get back on the gondola. I think that's enough for today. I have another idea."

# 15

## PAXTON

The closer we got to the hospital, the more nervous I got. Maybe that had something to do with Sera sitting next to me in the car. Snow began falling heavily as we walked into the large building.

"We're going to the hospital?" Sera said.

"I thought we could use some inspiration," I told her.

But now that we were walking toward the sliding front doors, my stomach was clenching with nerves.

I wasn't sure why I was reacting this way. I rarely got nervous for snowboarding competitions anymore. But maybe I was used to that kind of pressure.

This was different.

I wouldn't be riding a snowboard down a mountain, doing backflips and ollies. Instead, I was going to go visit the kids in the children's wing of the hospital.

I had called ahead to make sure it was okay, so when we got to the front desk, the nurse gave Sera a familiar greeting and then said, "Yes, Paxton, we're expecting you. The children's floor is on three. Elevators are down the hall and on the right."

I thanked the nurse and headed toward the elevators with Sera.

"I could make it here with my eyes closed," she admitted. "This place is as much home as the house I live in."

"That's how I feel about the slopes," I told her, feeling a kind of kinship.

Once we were in the elevator, she looked at me, an odd expression on her face.

"What?" I asked, wondering if I had a piece of lettuce in my teeth or something.

"Just... I think this is my first time hanging out with you in normal clothes, that's all. Instead of your snowboarding gear."

"Oh," I said with a laugh. "Gear is my 'normal'

clothes."

She smiled but couldn't respond before the elevator dinged, announcing we had reached the third floor.

The silver doors parted, and as we walked down the hallway, I studied the colorful walls. It had changed since my surgery, the walls showing new popular cartoon characters.

Past the lobby, we entered what seemed to be a playroom full of kids and some of their parents. I could tell they were parents from the way they fixed a kid's hair or gave them a hug.

Watching them, it kind of reminded me of my mom when I was growing up. She would fix my messy hair all the time, too.

That was before the divorce, back when we all still lived together. Now I got to see her in the off-season in South Carolina, where she lived with her new husband.

"You okay?" Sera asked, and I nodded.

She introduced me to everyone, and while a couple of the kids perked up at hearing my name, it was clear that most of them had no idea who I was.

A little boy with black curly hair and big

dark-brown eyes tugged on my shirt with his good arm that wasn't in a big cast. "Is it true you guys have a Christmas surprise for us?" His eyes glittered with excitement.

I glanced at Sera, whose mouth turned down slightly. I turned back to the boy. "We've got something for you, alright. But you're going to have to be a little patient until Christmas Eve, won't you?"

He and a little girl jumped up and down in excitement. "Christmas surprise, Christmas surprise!" They cried in unison.

I signed the casts of a couple of local snowboarders who knew me, and before I knew it, I had signed the cast of every kid in that room who had one. Other kids had signs of sickness like IV drips or burn marks. It made my heart ache because I knew they must be in pain.

So instead of just signing my name on their casts, I made sure to also write a short but encouraging note. Meanwhile, I couldn't help but notice that Sera didn't quite seem like herself. She wasn't joking or smiling with the kids. In fact, her expression seemed tense.

After a while, one of the nurses came in to

announce suppertime, saying that they would be showing a Christmas movie after.

Not wanting to interrupt, we said our good-byes and made our way back to the elevators.

"Are you okay? What's wrong?" I asked once the doors had closed us in.

She sighed. "I've been checking the numbers, Paxton. Things aren't looking good for the fundraiser."

I waited for her to go on. After a moment, she did, but this time her voice broke slightly.

"Even with all the calls and the flyers, we'll have enough for a candle and a–a Christmas story. That's all." She let her hands fall to her sides. "The one time I try to really do something meaningful and it doesn't seem like it's going to work."

I looked at my shoes, my chest feeling kind of heavy all of a sudden. I hadn't realized it was so dire when I made that promise to the kids.

The elevator doors opened and when we stepped out, Sera wiped at her eyes and said, "Sorry."

I grabbed her hand, wanting to ease the sadness I felt rolling off her.

She turned back to me, giving me a questioning look.

"We earned most of our money after the news segment, right?" I asked.

She nodded.

"I know you wanted to do this on your own, but let me post about it on my social media. We can make a video together that I bet we'll get some more money coming in for those kids. Especially if my friends share it around."

"Okay," she said, but she still sounded pretty disheartened.

I put my hand on her shoulder. "Hey, we're going to make this happen. I promise."

That seemed to get her attention, and it felt like her eyes were searching mine, trying to decide if she should believe me or not.

"Let's give it a try," she said.

So once we got outside, we stood in front of the hospital and I held up my phone while we took a video of us together talking about the fundraiser and how much money we had left to earn.

Before she had a chance to second guess it, I added the video to social media along with the Venmo username for donations.

"Done," I told her.

A small smile appeared on her face.

Selfishly, I wanted more of her smiles. I knew Dad would be upset with me for leaving the slopes early and coming home late, but I was also having trouble caring.

"Let's get some hot cocoa," I said. "My treat."

# PAXTON

When I got home, Dad was waiting for me.

"Where have you been?" he demanded as soon as I walked through the door, getting up from the kitchen table to meet me.

I knew he was gonna be upset with me. The entire way home, he'd been blowing up my phone with messages and phone calls.

He didn't bother tracking my location like some parents did.

After all, there were usually only three places I ever was: home, the gym, or the slopes. And most of the time, the answer was the slopes.

"I said, where have you been, Paxton?" he

repeated, barely giving me time to shut the front door and take off my coat.

He never called me Paxton, always Pax. He really was angry.

I began taking off my snow boots, not meeting his eyes. "I made a quick visit to the hospital in town for the fundraiser."

He walked toward me, his face clearly showing he was puzzled. "The hospital?"

I kicked off my boots and nodded. "Remember the fundraiser? There are several children there who are going to have to spend Christmas in a hospital room. Just thought I'd help cheer them up."

"This was supposed to be a small project, not something that would take you away from your training for hours on end," he huffed. "Is it about the fundraiser, or about the girl?"

My cheeks flamed as I glanced down. "I just thought I could help is all, Dad. I missed a few hours of practice one day. I won't do it again. No big deal."

That was the wrong thing to say. Now he looked even angrier. "No big deal? No big deal?"

I tried to walk past him to the fridge so I could get some food, but he blocked me.

"Paxton, you have a competition coming up in a matter of days. Missing a whole afternoon of practice? It's plain irresponsible. And it's not like you."

"Dad, it's fine," I mumbled. Finally, he let me pass him, and I opened the fridge, looking for food but too distracted to find anything.

He stood behind me, letting out a heavy sigh. "Maybe it's not such a good idea, being around this girl, Pax."

I closed the door and looked straight at him. "This isn't her fault, Dad. Going over there, it was my idea. And it was for a good cause. We're just trying to do something nice for those kids"

He didn't say anything.

"I'll be back on the slopes tomorrow, bright and early, okay?"

"Maybe it's for the best if you back off of the fundraiser, son. You can go back to what you do best, what you're meant to do. Which is to go out there and win. Make it to the Olympics. Then you'll have the money to make a real difference… Pax, listen to me. *Look* at me."

I exhaled, shutting the fridge and turning to face him.

"Do you know how rare it is to become an

Olympic athlete? Much less a medalist?" His voice became low, but still serious. "You're going to do it, son. I know you will. But now is not the time to lose focus. It's more important than ever that you practice, practice, practice."

I nodded, resigned. I knew he was right, but I couldn't stop the small tug in my chest that wanted *more*.

"Tell me you won't miss another practice," he said. "Promise me."

I looked at my dad, really looked at him. He seemed tired, stressed. And I remembered how much he had sacrificed so he could coach me and pay for all my gear and have time to take me to different competitions. This wasn't only about me.

"I promise I won't miss practice again," I said.

After searching my expression for a moment, he seemed satisfied with my response. "Go sit down. I'll get you some dinner."

A couple minutes later, he walked over to the table with a bowl full of chicken, rice, and vegetables. Our usual.

He sat down across from me as I began eating. I assumed he'd already had dinner while I was gone.

"You know, someone from the European circuit is going to be competing at the Christmas Eve meet, too. He wants to make a name for himself." Dad paused. "You're favored to win, which means you have a big target on your back. Now's the time to train harder. Especially with sponsors there looking for the next big name."

I took another bite, nodding along so he'd know I was listening.

"You've got to want it more than anyone else, Pax."

"I do." And if not, he wanted it enough for both of us.

Some days, I felt like he wanted me to get to the Olympics more than me. Like winning had become more important than anything else and was worth any cost.

Including losing Mom.

But it was never something we'd been able to talk about. Not really.

Dad pushed up from the table. "No more snowboarding with that girl, okay? You're doing good teaching her, but you need to push yourself harder, and she can't keep up on the courses you need to be on."

My eyebrows flew up. "You've been watching us?"

"It's my job to watch you," he said. "Finish your dinner and get some rest. I booked some sessions for you this week. Acupuncture, massage, and cupping. Your muscles will need to recover after the extra practice."

He left without another word.

# 17

## SERA

I watched my donations account grow along with the comments on Paxton's post. It wasn't enough to meet our goal, but it was enough to add another item to each gift basket.

I showed up to the slopes the next morning, excited to tell Paxton the news and keep discussing fundraising initiatives.

We were running out of time to raise enough for the special gift baskets I wanted to get, especially when we needed to put an order in advance. I didn't want to think about it, but Christmas Eve was just around the corner. We only had a few more days to make everything happen to order everything in time.

This was my first big project, the first thing I'd ever done on my own. Now I had Paxton's help, but still, it was my idea—ultimately my responsibility.

If I let those kids down, I'd never forgive myself.

And I'd probably never muster up the courage to do something like this ever again.

When I saw my friends again after the holidays, I wanted to be able to tell them what I had accomplished.

Unlike them, I didn't really have any hobbies or passions. They all had interests or something else going for them. I wanted to change that.

I found Paxton waiting for me near the main lodge like every other day. "Hey," I said.

He nodded at my greeting, but something looked off about him.

"Everything alright?" I asked. Without his usual megawatt smile, he almost looked sad.

He glanced away before looking back at me. "Listen, I–I can't practice with you today. I'm sorry."

"Oh," I stuttered. "Okay."

"My dad… I've got to stay on the blacks and

double diamonds today. My next competition is coming up soon and I've got to practice as much as I can."

I nodded quickly, looking down at the ground, hoping he couldn't sense the strange stinging in my eyes. "I understand." I wasn't very good after all. I just slowed him down.

"Please stay, though," he went on.

I looked up at him, searching his face for an explanation.

"Stay and get on the slopes. Practice what we've been doing. I'll check in later, maybe we can meet up before you head home and talk about the fundraiser."

My chest felt tight at the thought of snowboarding without Paxton encouraging me. But I also didn't want to go home and watch movies like I always used to. That's when I realized… I enjoyed my time on the slopes, and my time with Paxton.

"Okay," I said, finally. "I'll stay."

He smiled a little. "Good. Can I get your number? I don't have it or else I would have texted last night…"

My fingers fumbled over my phone surface as

I grabbed it from an internal zipper pocket. Then I passed it to him to type in his number.

He handed it back to me. "See you later?"

"Sure," I replied. "Break a leg."

He smiled fully now.

"Or don't, actually," I quipped.

"Deal," he said. "Well, stay safe." He left, going around the side of the lodge, and I stared after him for a second, realizing I already missed him.

Then I headed for the bunny slope. I did a couple of short practice runs, practicing my turns and stuff. Only falling once.

I smiled to myself, thinking that Paxton would've been happy to know it.

Feeling more confident, I went up the ski lift to take a green trail down. It was crazy to me that a week of practice was all it had taken to get more comfortable on a snowboard. I imagined coming out here next year and trying more challenging trails, with Paxton at my side.

On my run down the green, I saw someone ahead of me suddenly roll and crash hard.

I came to a stop as soon as I could, almost falling myself. When I turned back, I could see that whoever it was hadn't gotten back up yet.

Not a good sign.

I took one of my feet out of the board and hobbled over as fast as I could.

The guy had already taken his goggles off, and his face was etched in pain. He had to be younger than me, probably in middle school. He was just tall and kind of lanky. As I got closer, he tried to sit up, only to cry out in pain.

"Oh my gosh, are you okay?" I asked.

He shook his head. "I think it's broken, my leg."

I looked at his leg and gasped when I realized it was turned in a direction it shouldn't have been. My vision blurred for a moment, and my stomach turned.

Taking shallow breaths, I grabbed my phone from one of my zippered pockets. "I'm calling for help. Don't worry."

"Okay." He lay back down, breathing in short quick spurts. His voice was a whimper as he asked, "Can I hold your hand?"

"Of course." I offered my gloved hand for him, and he squeezed it tightly.

With my free hand, I quickly went to the lodge website and found the emergency hotline.

A few rings later, I gave them the details of what had happened and where we were, holding the boy's hand all the while.

"They'll be here soon," I promised him. I wished I could do more for him, especially when tears began rolling down his cheeks.

"What's your name?" I asked.

He kept breathing quickly. "Jared."

"You're going to be okay, Jared," I told him. "I promise. My mom's a doctor at the hospital."

"Really?" That seemed to cheer him up a bit.

I nodded. "And my dad's a nurse. I'll let them know to take extra good care of you."

Soon, the roar of a snowmobile's engine filled the air. Two snowmobiles. The ski resort medics loaded him carefully onto a stretcher and pulled him behind him. Gone just like that.

I watched them disappear, rattled at how everything had happened so fast.

I realized I had been crying, too, now that it was all over.

As I carefully snowboarded back to the main lodge, I realized why I was crying. That boy would likely end up in the hospital over the holidays, with that bad of a break.

I could still feel the ghost of him squeezing

my hand, picture the tears in his eyes. Now more than ever, I felt determined to set my pride aside and make a difference this holiday season.

Every single patient in that hospital deserved it.

# 18

# PAXTON

After hours of practice, my runs down the slope began to blur together. When I got to the bottom this time, I checked my watch, seeing it was way past lunchtime. I still hadn't checked in with Sera.

"Good," Dad said, coming up to me. "You're looking sharp."

"Thanks, Dad," I said.

"You have lunch yet?" he asked.

I shook my head. "No, not yet."

"Come on, we'll get a quick bite then head back to the practice course. I'll grab the tripod so we can record you and watch it back tonight."

"I was hoping to eat lunch with Sera," I told him. "She should be around here."

"No, we need to talk about your ollies over lunch. That was your biggest point deduction last time."

Every point mattered in his eyes. Even when I was coming in first place.

I followed him back to our cabin. The whole time he gave me advice, pointers, things I already knew and that he'd told me a thousand times.

When I walked in behind him and took off my gear, I was fed up. "Okay, Dad. I know, okay?" My words came out sharper than I'd ever spoken to him before.

He stared at me.

My chest moved up and down, from the frustration I felt inside, but I didn't say anything else.

Neither did he.

He probably already knew what this was about.

I needed time with Sera, to work on the fundraiser. That was important, too.

Not just snowboarding.

I couldn't let that be my whole life anymore.

"You're throwing a fit about that girl?" he asked.

I blew out my breath, not wanting to lose my temper at his use of the word "fit," like I was a naughty child. I was almost eighteen. "I'm tired of this," I admitted, my voice cracking.

"When you want to the be the best, Pax, you have to make sacrifices sometimes."

He didn't sound like he was mad. In fact, there was emotion to his voice. My snowboarding career had cost him, too. Dad could have had a higher-up position at the ski lodge, but instead he taught morning lessons to make money so he could spend all afternoon with me.

I felt a little guilty as I looked at him and nodded.

"When you're an Olympian, then you can take a break. You have this small window where your actions matter *so* much. I don't want to see you waste it."

So the whole afternoon, I kept practicing, kept improving, until my body was so spent I just wanted to pass out in bed.

But I also thought about the fundraiser and how I could help even though I didn't have much time to give, at least right now. On the short drive home, I checked in with Sera, finally. She told me about her day, how she'd helped some kid who'd had a bad accident on the slopes. It sounded really grizzly.

Paxton: That's terrible. I'm glad you were there to help him.

After that, I sent her a clip one of my snowboarding friends had texted me.

Someone on the slopes had recorded us snowboarding together, and the video had gone viral.

Sera: Whoa, a million likes? That's insane!
Paxton: Insane in a good way, if we can find a way to make it work for the fundraiser. What do you think?

A minute later, she texted back.

Sera: I think it's worth a shot.

I thought about what my dad had said earlier.

Paxton: You should use it to make videos about the fundraiser. Use more clips of us. Whatever you gotta do to get people donating. I'll post it on my social.
Sera: I don't think they love the video because of

me... They like seeing YOU do a good thing. Like teaching a lost cause to snowboard.

I chuckled to myself. She clearly wasn't a lost cause because when I caught a glimpse of her boarding earlier, she was holding her own.

Paxton: What do you think we should do then?
Sera: Try going live on your social media channel tonight. Talk to your followers and tell them why it matters. You're our best shot.

I scanned her words. Even though I was just reading them, I could imagine her disappointed tone. Sera felt like she was living in everyone's shadow, but that wasn't true. She was the one who started this whole thing. So I sent her a message back.

Paxton: Teamwork makes the dream work. :)

I liked the thought of Sera and I being teammates in this. Maybe one day we could be something more.

# SERA

Paxton went live on his channel for half an hour before bed last night and raised almost enough money to add another item to the gift basket. Immediately after he got off the live, I called him so we could plan for the next one.

He wanted me to meet him at the lodge during his lunch break the following day. Somehow, he'd convinced his dad to give him half an hour if he agreed to talk with him after dinner. And we decided we would do our next live then. So, I brought the items we were adding to the baskets to show people and a list of things we had on our wish list to add if we raised more money.

Paxton fiddled with his phone, getting ready to go live. He didn't have much time, and we wanted to make the most of it. I stayed across the table from him while he hooked his phone into the tripod, but then he said, "Come here. You should be live with me."

My heartrate ramped up at the thought of being on camera. "That's okay. They want to see you, anyway."

He shook his head. "Everyone should meet the person behind the fundraiser," he told me. His tone left no room for argument.

So I sat next to him, our shoulders brushing. I could smell *outside* on his clothes, something I was getting used to after so much time on the mountainside.

Soon, he'd pushed the red button, and a countdown started until the screen revealed a message saying we were live.

There was a wave of people in the comments asking who I was. Of course, plenty of people knew who Paxton Smith was. Most of the people in the comments were girls who had huge crushes on him and wanted to know if I was his girlfriend.

Paxton blushed a little, and so did I.

"We're just friends," I said. "So don't worry. But maybe what we should do is give away a date with Paxton to the highest donor. What do you think, everyone?" I asked.

Paxton sputtered at the idea even though all of his followers were asking where they could donate.

"It would help a lot of kids," I teased him. "Be a good sport, come on." I turned back to the camera. "How many of you would love to go on a date with Paxton Smith?"

The live erupted with hearts and comments.

Paxton said, "There's only one girl I want to date, so I'll have to pass. Sera, can you share the link to the fundraiser again?"

My stomach fluttered as I typed it out, wondering if he'd been talking about me. Wishful thinking. I tried to focus while he started talking more about the kids at the hospital. At first, I wasn't entirely sure why he wanted to help so badly, but the way he spoke about the kids, I could tell he truly cared about making their holidays better.

"Garland Memorial Hospital serves lots of local and visiting guests here in our town. It's been around for over a hundred years. And every year, the hospital does whatever they can to make the patients have the best holiday season they can. But it's not easy. The holidays can be lonely for a lot of people, and it's even more true when you're a kid far away from home and hurting from an injury or illness," he said.

More hearts filled the screen.

"It was really Sera's idea," Paxton said, gesturing that I should talk.

His acknowledgement made me feel warm inside. My smile came naturally as I said, "I want to make the kids at the hospital feel like they're not missing out on Christmas. So Paxton and I got some things to bring Christmas to them."

We showed the book and air freshener we'd raised money for so far and some items on the wish list

Paxton chimed in. "What's your favorite part of Christmas? Tell me in the comments."

He began reading comments out loud. I encouraged people to donate.

One person said they would donate fifty dollars if Paxton sang *Jingle Bells* and danced while he did it.

The comments were coming so fast I couldn't even read them all. Numbers showing the amount of people watching ticked up and up, doubling by the time he was done with the song.

I laughed and told people to come up with more silly ideas.

He sang a couple more Christmas tunes and even pretended to be one of Santa's elves for a while. But his dad came into the break room, tapping his wrist to let Paxton know he had to get back to practice.

"We better get going," Paxton said. "Thanks for hanging out with us and donating to a good cause!"

"Thank you, everyone," I echoed.

I saw several people comment how much they loved that Paxton was doing his part to give back to the community as we signed off. As soon as it said the live was ended, I checked the fundraising account.

"Oh my gosh!" I cried out, not believing the number I was seeing.

Paxton was already pulling his gear back on, but he dropped his boots to come see what I was staring at. "What is it?" he asked.

I showed him the number on the screen. "Look how much we raised in less than an hour!"

He smiled too, and pretty soon, we were both laughing and jumping up and down.

"This is absolutely incredible," I said, thinking back to that fateful day when that guy had crashed into my fundraiser booth. "I really couldn't have done this without you, you know. Thank you."

"You would've found a way," Paxton replied. "But I'm glad I get to help anyway."

I thought about what we could do with the extra money. "This is enough to cover another item for the gift basket."

"Good," he said. "Then we should do more lives."

I nodded, agreeing right away.

Paxton remained pretty close to me, and I almost asked him what he meant when he said there was only one girl he wanted to date.

Instead, the door opened, and his dad walked in. "Pax, what's the hold up?"

Paxton tore his gaze away from me, and I got busy gathering up my things.

"Sorry, Dad. Lost track of time." He grabbed his gear and looked back at me for a second before following his dad out the door.

# PAXTON

followed Dad back to the slopes where a permanent course was set up for training. I knew he was upset with me for going late on the live because he walked almost too fast for me to keep up in my snowboard boots. These things weren't the easiest to walk in.

"Dad, just say it," I finally said as he stopped by the course to set up his tripod.

"Pax, you know I hate to keep saying this, but you're giving me no other choice." He turned to face me. "This girl, all of this, it's a distraction, and it's going to start costing you competitions. First, it's skipping practice, then it's going late on lunch. What's next? Getting injured because you're distracted?"

I sighed. Once he got started, there wasn't much I could do to stop him.

"You've got to focus, Paxton. But I can't make you. It's not like when you were little and you needed reminders to pay attention. You're old enough now that you need to know for yourself why it's important to show up and show up on time."

"Okay, Dad, I'm sorry," I mumbled.

I knew that if I didn't say something, the lecture would only get worse.

Dad exhaled. "You promised—" He paused, starting over. "You've worked too hard to mess things up now with so many sponsors watching you." His chest rose up and down for a second as he continued looking at me. "I just want you to see what you can do. You can get equipment sponsors, training sponsors, reach the Olympics, but only if you don't lose focus now when we're *this* close."

I cleared my throat, shame washing over me. "I know, Dad. You're right. I'll—I'll do better, I promise." I'd seen people get horrible injuries from being distracted, and I didn't want to be one of them. Years of hard work, an entire future career, gone in an instant.

I went to the top of the run and went through it, determined to do my best. I had to show Dad and myself that I could have a life outside of snowboarding while still being a good, dedicated athlete.

After a couple passes, Dad stopped me and gave me some things to work on. I worked on them again and again and again until he had nothing else to say about my form or my turns or anything else.

I made sure to stay as long as Dad wanted to make up for the time I'd missed earlier, so the sun was setting by the time Dad finally said we should go home for dinner.

Once I went inside, got my gear off, and finally sat on my bed, I pulled out my phone.

There was a text from Sera waiting for me.

Sera: Sorry about your dad. Is everything okay?

I sighed, trying to think of how to say what I needed to say next.

It was a while before I was able to type it out.

Paxton: Listen, I'm sorry, but I've got to focus on snowboarding for a while. My next competition is on Christmas Eve. I can be there on Christmas to help you deliver gifts when this competition is over. Let me give you the password to my account so you can make any posts you want about the fundraiser.

I fired it off and then put my phone away, knowing Sera would be disappointed. I was disappointed, too. It seemed like no matter what I chose to do, I'd fail at least one person.

When I got to the dinner table, Dad began talking about the other snowboarders I'd be up against and what I needed to know so that I could beat them.

At the end of the day, this was what mattered. Winning.

Helping people felt good–and maybe I really could do more once I had more notoriety.

That's what I tried to tell myself anyway, especially when I kept thinking that I was letting Sera down.

# 21
## SERA

Considering how upset I was when Paxton volunteered for my project on the local news, I was even more disappointed when he said he had to focus on snowboarding instead.

I understood how important snowboarding and practice was to him, but I missed hanging out with him. He was so patient and even-keeled compared to me, who tended to overthink everything.

Like right now.

I couldn't help but wonder how he was doing, if his practices were going okay... if he missed me at all.

Even though part of me didn't want to admit it, I missed training with him. Riding the ski lift beside him and looking over to see his smile, the mountains reflected in his mirrored goggles.

"Honey, are you okay?" Dad asked from the love seat where he and Mom were sitting across from me in the living room.

They both had a rare night off leading up to the holidays, but only because they were both scheduled for Christmas Eve and Christmas Day. We'd eaten dinner together and then they put on our favorite movie, Elf.

We always laughed hardest at the scene of him putting syrup on his spaghetti because I'd tried to do that one year after seeing the movie. I'd been so little then. This year, I could hardly smile.

No wonder Dad was worried about me.

I gave him a half smile. "I'm okay. Just tired."

He didn't look convinced, but he didn't press the issue any further.

Meanwhile, Mom gave a light snore, her head on his shoulder. She always fell asleep halfway through a movie—or if she sat in one place too long. Dad looked about ready to pass out as well.

He gave me a sheepish look, his silent apology for Mom.

"You don't need to worry about me," I said, turning back to the TV, even though I wasn't really paying attention to the movie. I'd seen Elf about a hundred million times. I practically knew it by heart.

Dad got up and gave me a hug and a kiss on the forehead. "Good night, kiddo. I promise we'll be more fun next time."

"Night." I gave him a playful salute and watched him gently wake her up and walk with her to bed.

While the movie played, I picked up my phone and scrolled on social media. It wasn't long before the viral video of Paxton and me came up on my feed.

His happy grin while snowboarding with me made me smile as I watched him on the screen. The joy on his face was contagious. My chest gave a pang, thinking of him. I tried not to think too much about what it meant.

Instead, I scrolled to the comments. There were over a hundred there. Most of them had to do with how much they wished Paxton could give them lessons, but then I spotted a comment about me.

Smartyp: What's HE doing with HER? Doesn't he know he could do better?

Reading the words stung, but for some reason, I didn't put my phone down. Some sort of masochistic force had me skimming through the comments even faster.

Pretty soon, I found a couple more comments like it. About me. Saying unkind things about my weight or my face or my snowboarding skills, things that made my face burn red.

I watched the video again, and now that I'd found those comments, I couldn't help but notice how I looked compared to Paxton.

He was good looking, with his perfectly charming smile, perfect hair, and fit body.

Then there was me, with my messy hair and my curves visible even with ultra-thick snow gear. I practically looked like a marshmallow next to Paxton.

Finally, I threw my phone onto the love seat a few feet away where my parents had been sitting.

I'd been kidding myself when I said we were

only friends on that live. I was crushing on him, hard. But according to all those people, I'd never measure up to deserve a guy like Paxton.

Just another thing I'd failed to do.

A tear rolled down my cheek, and I let it fall. More followed as I walked to my bedroom and shut the door behind me.

# 22
## PAXTON

*I* was supposed to be sleeping, but I couldn't sleep no matter how hard I tried.

With the amount of hours I'd practiced that day, I should've been out the second my head hit the pillow. But even though my body was exhausted, my mind wouldn't stop buzzing with thoughts of Sera and the fundraiser. Reaching our goal was a stretch with the lives, but now that Dad wanted me to back off of it? We wouldn't make it.

I checked the time again and sighed.

*Two hours.* Two hours I'd been trying to sleep and failing.

At this rate, I'd be lucky to get a few precious

hours of sleep before it was time to put my mind and body through rigorous training all over again.

After rolling over one more time and failing to sleep all over again, I finally turned my lamp back on. I lay there for a minute, staring at the ceiling. Then I picked up my phone and texted Sera.

I had to know how she was doing, how the fundraiser was going.

It was killing me not being able to help her.

Or see her.

But at least I could talk to her.

Paxton: Hey

I watched the screen, hoping maybe she was awake, too. That maybe she'd been thinking of me as much as I'd thought of her.

A minute later, while I was still staring up at the ceiling, my phone dinged with a text back.

Sera: Hey

Dots appeared on my screen, and a second later, another text.

Sera: You're up late.

I texted right back.

Paxton: I am. Couldn't sleep. How are things going?

Dots appeared on the screen again. They disappeared and reappeared a few times before her text finally rolled in.

Sera: I don't know

My brows pinched as I studied her message.

Paxton: Is everything okay? Anything I can help with?
Sera: I'm not sure.

My brows knit together in confusion. Huh?

Paxton: Try me.

Three dots came up on the screen, and they stayed there for a while until her message finally came through.

Sera: I just feel like you're the only reason I raised any money at all. I'm just a nobody with a dumb dream. A charity case.

I read that last part again, dumbfounded.

Paxton: A charity case? No way are you a charity case.

She didn't say anything else for a minute, and more than anything, I wished I was in the same room as her so I could do more than try to cheer her up via text message.

Sera: I'll always just be Dr. Lopez's daughter. I'll never be seen as anything more. If I haven't figured out who I'm supposed to be by now, something I'm good at, I just don't think I'll ever be able to do it.

That made me think about myself and how from a young age I knew I loved snowboarding. I'd been good at it. Really good. Good enough that my dad had quit his corporate job and made coaching me his entire life's mission.

Now I was over here wishing I could trade my life for hers.

A life with two parents who still loved each other. Time to do whatever I wanted.

What was that saying about the grass being greener?

I waited to see if Sera would say anything else, but she didn't.

I read over the last message she sent, trying to think of something I could say that might show her how cool I thought she was.

Paxton: I see you as more than Dr. Lopez's daughter, Sera.

I wanted to type more, how she was funny and always knew what to say to break the ice. She was kind, proven by her fundraising idea and the fact that she kept going, even when getting plowed over by a rogue snowboarder. That made her persistent, too. She didn't give up on the fundraiser or on snowboarding. She shouldn't give up on herself, either.

Maybe I'd tell her that, depending on her reply.

Problem was, she texted back this:

Sera: I'm sorry, I need to go. Goodnight.

# 23
## SERA

The next morning, Mom came into the living room wearing her scrubs for her shift. Her dark hair was pulled into a bun and tortoiseshell glasses rested on her broad nose.

I was snuggled into the couch, a thick warm blanket around me while a Christmas movie played on the TV. With Christmas just five days away, tomorrow morning was my deadline to put in the final order for the gift basket. They weren't going to be as big as I'd hoped for, but something was better than nothing.

At least, that's what I told myself so I wouldn't break down in tears.

Mom came into the room, using an app on her phone to shut off the TV.

Confused, I sat up to face her. "What was that for?"

Lines formed on her forehead as she sat next to me. "You seem off. What's going on?"

I shrugged and gave a small sigh while staring at the black TV screen. "Things aren't going the way I thought they would."

"You mean with the fundraiser?" she clarified.

I nodded.

Mom bit her lip. She was wearing her favorite scrubs with stars and moons on the front pocket underneath her name embroidered in midnight blue letters. She had almost worked for NASA before going the med school route. That's how much of a genius she was.

She'd had her choice of NASA or going to Harvard Medical. Both had wanted her.

A wicked voice in my mind wondered if she was disappointed to have me as a daughter.

Mom patted my knee. "You know what helps me when I'm feeling down?"

I wondered when the last time she must have felt down was. Maybe the last time she hadn't outperformed everyone she knew?

Mom shook my leg. "Hey, Earth to Sera, Earth to Sera. Did you hear me?"

I looked at her. "Huh?"

"I said, you know what helps me feel better when I'm down?"

I waited for her to go on.

"Throwing myself into service. Helping others. It always does the trick, I promise," she went on.

"But the stupid fundraiser is why I'm feeling down," I protested. "I tried helping others and I couldn't even do that right."

Mom's watch dinged on her wrist, and she looked at it with a frown. "I'm sorry, I have to go." She stood back up, looking back at me again. "There's always someone in need, Sera. Go see what Mrs. Mulberry is up to. She's always looking for volunteers this time of year. Promise?"

I let out a sigh. "Promise."

For a while, I thought about breaking my word and just staying home, but I wanted Mom to be right. I wanted to feel better.

When I looked in the mirror, my hair gave me a jump-scare. After wrangling it into a long braid, I grabbed my coat and headed to Santa's

Elves on foot. *Maybe I just wasn't meant to be a leader,* I thought. *I could be a helper, though.*

The weather was bitingly cold, but it felt good to breathe fresh air. I hated to admit it, but Mom was onto something, getting me out of the house.

In no time, I was walking into the old house that was home to Santa's Elves. A few volunteers were spread out in the living room with boxes of toys and clothes and shoes. They wore cute red and green vests and hats as they wrapped presents for local families who didn't have money for gifts this year.

A familiar voice called to me from the kitchen. "Sera, is that you?"

I gave her a wave and walked over to her. She was sitting at a table, some type of paperwork spread in front of her. "Hi, Mrs. Mulberry. Merry Christmas."

"And a merry Christmas to you." She set down her pen and folded her hands on the table. "And what can I do for you today?"

All of a sudden, my hands felt like they had nothing to do. I shoved them in my pockets. "Actually, I had some time, so I was hoping I could pitch in around here. Make up for that broken booth. What can I do to help?"

I didn't have to ask Mrs. Mulberry twice. There was always something to do at Santa's Elves.

A couple hours later, I had wrapped about a hundred Christmas presents. Everything from fuzzy socks and flannel blankets to dolls and action figures. There wasn't much room in the living room, so I went to one of the "bedrooms" to work. It had been converted to a giftwrapping storage area with rolls of wrapping paper lining the walls with ribbon, tape, scissors, and labels.

I hadn't realized how much time had passed until Mrs. Mulberry checked in on me, bringing me a bottle of water. "How's it going?" she asked. "Anything you need."

It was wild that she was doing so much for the community and still checking in on me. I was in awe of this woman and all she did. Especially considering the massive stack of presents she was donating. I'd never seen these many gifts in my life.

Mrs. Mulberry smiled as she looked around. "Thank you for helping today, Sera. These gifts are going to the most needy in Garland as well as the surrounding areas. Santa's Elves is making sure every child within a hundred miles will have a Christmas this year. You're a part of that now."

Her voice became emotional as she said it, and I couldn't help but feel tears in my eyes as I thought about the impact she was making.

I turned to her. "You've been running this place a long time, haven't you?"

She smiled again and sat down next to me on the floor. She was older but still spry. "I've been at this a long time, yes. Three decades, in fact."

"Wow," I said. "Think about how many families you've helped."

She touched my hand. "It never ceases to amaze me what's possible when you set your mind to it."

I blinked at the floor, thinking about how determined I'd felt about the fundraiser in the beginning. Now, more than ever, I just felt deflated. Tears brimmed in my eyes. Maybe I just didn't have what someone like Mrs. Mulberry had.

She squeezed my hand. "What is it, love?" she asked.

"I just—I just thought maybe if I set *my* mind to it, I'd be able to accomplish something I could be proud of this year," I confided. A tear ran down my cheek.

"The hospital fundraiser. I thought it was a wonderful idea."

"Yeah, but I couldn't pull it off like I wanted to. I'm worried all I'll ever be is a helper. I think that's all I'm good at."

Mrs. Mulberry squeezed my shoulder this time. "You know, I keep hearing you say I, I, I. No one can do anything on their own, Sera, not really. Not something like this."

I tried to think about what she was saying. I noticed just how many volunteers were around us.

"That's why charities exist, Sera," she reminded me. "Not to prove yourself or earn your place in this world. Charities exist to support people when they're down. One person couldn't possibly do it all on their own."

I nodded, starting to understand what she was saying.

Mrs. Mulberry stood up, stretching out her knees and back. "I bet if you look around, you'll see you're not alone in this. And it's worth the smiles on those kids' faces to get a little help."

# PAXTON

Dad walked into the kitchen, a big grin on his face. I hadn't seen him this happy since before the divorce.

I swallowed my bite of breakfast and asked, "What's going on?"

He came over to me and clapped me on the back. "I think we did it."

"Did what?" I questioned, wiping my mouth with a napkin. He'd been locked away in his office, on the phone for over an hour even though it was still early in the morning.

"We have a sponsor meeting," he said, going to pour himself another cup of coffee. After taking a sip, he leaned back on the counter.

"They're looking for an Olympic hopeful to invest in. They've been watching your tapes and think you're it."

My jaw dropped. I hadn't even gone to the qualifying event yet–that wouldn't be until January.

"I thought this was a scouting trip," I said to Dad. We knew a lot of potential sponsors would be at the Christmas Eve competition.

"It may be for others, but these guys are the real deal." Dad sounded practically giddy. "They're looking at a deal to sponsor gear and training with an agreement for you to participate in next year's marketing campaign. He wants to talk to you to make sure you're a good fit, but I think with a bit of luck, we've got it in the bag."

"Wow, that's great, Dad." Though I didn't feel as relieved as him. Dad had been talking non-stop about finding me a sponsor. More than ever, we needed money for travel, entry fees, room and board, more coaching and training. If I didn't do well in this interview, would we be able to find a different sponsor?

I also wasn't naive. I knew he'd sacrificed, made trades, and used up all of our savings on my snowboarding career. Every spare penny had been going to this dream for years. But having a sponsor, and a big one, well that could change everything for us.

"When do they want to talk to me?" I asked, getting up and leaning on the counter.

"I told him you could talk today. The video call is scheduled for a couple hours. Pax, this would set us up for a long time. I'm not just talking better gear and more competitions. I'm talking college and beyond, son. I wouldn't have to teach lessons anymore. I could be your full-time coach."

I raised my brows. "Sounds like a lot of money."

"They're betting on you," he said. "They've seen you compete, and they think you could be the next Shaun White."

I blew out a breath. "Wow." If I was going to get a sponsor this big, Dad was right. I needed to be more committed and focused than ever. "Okay," I said, nodding. "I'll talk to them. You can count on me."

He clapped me on the shoulder again. "I knew I could count on you, Pax."

The time to meet rolled around before I felt

even close to being ready. As my stomach turned, I was glad I hadn't finished my breakfast earlier.

Sure, I'd talked to small sponsors before, reporters from time to time, but nothing like this. I checked my appearance in the bathroom mirror one more time before heading to Dad's office.

Dad patted the chair next to him, and I joined him.

He gave me a few last-minute pointers and then we were on the video call. This was more nerve-racking than anything I'd done on a snowboard.

A guy around my dad's age, wearing a suit and tie with short brown hair, came on the screen. They immediately greeted each other, and before long, Dad introduced me to John Pemberly, the director of sponsorship and community outreach at a very big winter gear company.

Strangely, I did most of the talking. Jon asked me questions about school and my friends. I got the sense that he wanted to see what kind of person I was. If I would be a good fit to represent a company like theirs.

Dad had said as much before the call. They

didn't just want someone with talent. At my level, talent was everywhere. But they wanted to know if I had a good head on my shoulders.

"You know, I like you, Paxton," John said. "A lot. But more than ever, we're looking for athletes who don't just win. We want someone who stands for something. Who goes above and beyond, not just on the field, but in their local community."

I swallowed. Now the interview had really begun.

"Tell me. Are you involved in any charity work? I know you have a busy training schedule, but do you ever volunteer or get involved in local projects?" he asked.

I glanced at Dad, who had noticeably paled and gone silent for the first time on the call.

Smiling, I turned back to the man on the screen. "Actually, I'm glad you asked, because I have been involved in a very special project this year." I told him all about meeting Sera on the first day of her fundraiser and how we'd worked together since. "Getting to be a part of it has really given me a lot of perspective on who I want to be as an athlete and as a person. We might not make it to our fundraising goal, but Sera and I have worked really hard to make it happen while sticking with my training schedule."

Jon grinned at me. "I love the sound of this project. And I love that you're the kind of young man who saw an opportunity and decided to do something about it. That's what's missing from a lot of young people these days."

I glanced at Dad again, who smiled a little sheepishly.

"I want you to keep me updated on this fundraiser," Jon said, "and I want you to know, we will be making a contribution. I'm also going to put you in touch with our director of social media marketing. She's an absolute whiz. I know she'd be happy to give you two some pointers on how to get this fundraiser to the finish line, all while getting your name out there."

"Thank you!" I blustered. "Really, that would be incredible." I could just picture the weight lifting from Sera's shoulders when she found out that we might just reach our goal, and how happy the kids at the hospital would be to see their baskets on Christmas morning.

"Happy to help," Jon said. "We'll be sending an official sponsorship agreement for you and your dad to look over once the project is complete. I want to keep seeing what you can do."

"Thank you, sir." I replied. "Thank you very much."

Jon smiled back. "I think this is going to be the start of a beautiful partnership, Paxton."

We got off the call, and Dad turned to me.

He wrapped me in a big hug, and it was a second before I realized what was happening. I hugged him back.

Finally, he let go and looked at me, his eyes red and moist. "You did it. I knew you could do it, Pax."

"Thanks, Dad," I said with a grin. I cleared my throat of the frog that was threatening to creep in.

"I'm proud of you son," he said, "Not just this, but the fundraiser, as well. With all we've given to snowboarding, it's hard for me to remember other things matter, too."

He stood up and exhaled, clearly still full of adrenaline like me.

Before he left, he turned to me. "You make sure you call Sera today. Make sure she knows you'll be around to help again. It's important. And I won't question your commitment to snowboarding again."

I cleared my throat again. "Thanks, Dad. That means a lot."

# 25

# SERA

When I saw Mom come in from the garage that night, I ran up to her and hugged her.

She laughed and hugged me back. "Whoa, what's this for?"

I stayed nuzzled in her shoulder. "For being the best mom ever."

She scoffed. "I know that can't be true. I work way too many hours for that to ever be true."

Her voice broke as she said it, and I looked up at her. "You're still a great mom. Not just a really good doctor."

That made her cry, and then I was crying, too. Mom never cried. She was always too focused on her work and her patients. All this time, I thought she must be perfect and know it. Now I could see even she had her struggles.

We went to the kitchen to get a box of tissues. "So, what brought this on?"

I dabbed at my eyes as I sat at the table across from her. "I went to see Mrs. Mulberry like you suggested. Mom, it was great." I told her all about what I'd done at Santa's Elves. Everything Mrs. Mulberry was doing, plus what she had told me. "I feel like I've been going about this all wrong," I admitted, my cheeks feeling hot. "I felt like I could use this fundraiser to prove I was good on my own, not just because I was 'Dr. Lopez's daughter'. But that was selfish. I shouldn't have factored into the fundraising at all; it's about making Christmas better for those kids."

Mom's eyes shined as she nodded. "She's got a lot of wisdom that Mrs. Mulberry."

I nodded. "I think I'm going to keep volunteering there. There's a lot I can learn from her."

She touched my cheek. "Good," she said. "I worry about you sometimes, being by yourself all the time."

"I'm not," I told her. "I've got my friends. And

now, Mrs. Mulberry. And Paxton," I added, feeling myself blush. "I mean, if he wants to see me when school starts back up."

Our last conversation hadn't gone so well. I'd been at a low point and had been short with him. That wasn't who I wanted to be.

Before Mom could ask about Paxton, I added, "Plus I know I've got you and Dad, too." I took a breath. "That being said... will you email your doctor friends about my fundraiser?"

Mom gave me a knowing smile. "Absolutely." She got up and kissed the top of my head. "I'm going to go shower and get to bed. I'm absolutely exhausted. See you in the morning?"

"See you in the morning," I replied.

Once I was alone in the kitchen, I got out my phone and texted Paxton.

Sera: Hey. I'm sorry about the other day. I was having a hard time, and I just want you to know, it wasn't your fault.

A few minutes later, he texted me back.

Paxton: Meet me in town for hot cocoa tomorrow morning?

I stared at his message. That was it?

Sera: What time?
Paxton: Does 9 work?

My eyebrows pinched together. Wasn't he supposed to be practicing in the mornings? He'd said he needed to focus for that big competition on Christmas Eve.

But instead of looking a gift horse in the mouth, I tapped out my reply.

Sera: I'll see you there.

AFTER TAMING my hair and putting on a little lip gloss, I sent a text to let my parents know where I was headed.

They were both sleeping in before their shift later today, but that was okay because I was going to be busy myself. There wasn't a lot of time left for fundraising, and I was going to earn as much as I could before placing my final order from Santa's Bag.

My heart fluttered anxiously as I approached

Cider Center and then crossed the street to Cocoa Corner. I was excited to see Paxton, but at the same time, I wasn't sure what he thought of me after our last conversation.

Bells chimed over the door as I walked in, and then I saw Paxton sitting at a booth with two large cocoas. For a split second before he looked up, I just took him in. He wore regular clothes today–jeans and a sweater with a beanie atop his shaggy blond hair. His side profile was so handsome, with his strong chin and sharp nose. His eyes were on his hands as he twisted the cup in front of him.

But then those eyes landed on me.

I expected a wave, maybe a smile if I was lucky. But then he got up and opened his arms for a hug.

"Hey," I said as I folded myself into his arms. It felt good to be here, to have my cheek against his strong chest. Even if it lasted far too short for my liking.

"It's good to see you," he said as we sat down.

"Yeah," I said over the lump in my throat. "Feels like forever."

I wasn't sure the exact reason why he asked me to meet him here, but I had to say something first. "Listen, I really am sorry about the other night."

Paxton put down his hot cocoa. "It's okay. You've got nothing to apologize for, I promise."

I glanced down and bit my lip, still feeling a little embarrassed. My friends were the only people I usually got so vulnerable with. But Paxton had shown me he was a friend I could trust. "I know we don't have a lot of time, but I've enlisted help with the fundraiser so we can get the word out. I'm done trying to act like I can do this all on my own."

"That's great," Paxton said. "But actually, I wanted to meet you here because I have some news of my own."

"Really? What is it?" I took a sip of my cocoa, thinking of our time at the ice bar together.

"Have you checked the fundraiser account this morning?" he asked.

I looked at him over my mug, confused. "No, why?"

"Go check." A small smile played along his lips.

Excited nerves made my hands shake as I set my mug back down and reached for my phone.

When I saw the number in my app, I stared at him. "Oh my gosh! How?"

He grinned. "My new sponsor wanted to make a donation."

I was speechless. My mouth opened and closed as I vacillated between congratulating him on the new sponsor and thanking him for talking about our fundraiser. "Wow," I said finally. "Paxton, that's amazing." I looked at the number again, still processing. "This means we're going to buy all of the gift baskets, with everything on our wish list."

He nodded. "Yeah, it does."

As I looked at my phone, more money started coming in. Mom's doctor friends must be donating, too. I put my phone on the table and slid it to him so he could see, still in disbelief. "Oh my gosh." My voice shook with emotion.

Paxton came around to my side of the booth and sat next to me, hugging me again.

"I couldn't have done this without you," I cried as I held on to him.

"I'm glad we could do this together," he told me. "I think it's my best Christmas yet."

I smiled through the tears as I pulled away.

Gently, he wiped one of the tears away with his thumb.

His gaze flicked to my lips, and I thought he might kiss me. But then the bell over the door clanged loudly and we jumped apart.

After a beat, Paxton said, "Sounds like we've got some baskets to order."

I laughed. "We do."

# 26

# PAXTON

Snowboarding in the Christmas Eve competition wasn't just fun and invigorating like most competitions... It was fulfilling.

For the first time ever, I felt like I was snowboarding for something that was bigger than just myself. I saw how my talent and hard work could influence more than the final score; it could change the world. Winning and finalizing my sponsorship felt like an achievement instead of a requirement.

I had Sera to thank for that–and the guy who crashed into her. But we didn't want to give him too much credit.

So when I woke up on Christmas morning, I was excited for more than presents. I was pumped to deliver Christmas baskets to the kids at the hospital.

Dad was sipping hot black coffee when I made it to the kitchen, buzzing with energy before I even had my regular energy drink.

"Merry Christmas, Pax," Dad said, giving me a hug. "You ready to head out?"

He was dropping me off at the hospital to meet Sera, and she would give me a ride home later. When we got to our destination, I thanked him for the ride and reached for the handle, but Dad put a hand on my arm. "Wait."

I looked back at him, and for a second I was worried he'd tell me to hurry up so we could get more practice in. But his eyes crinkled around the corners. "I'm proud of you."

My chest swelled. He had always told me good job or commented on my improvements. But this was the first time, in a long time, I'd heard the P-word. Somehow, it meant more that it had nothing to do with snowboarding.

"I love you," I told him.

"Love you, too." He sounded a little choked up, and I couldn't blame him. There was a small lump forming in my throat, too.

I swallowed it as I walked through the entry

doors to the hospital to find Sera waiting in the lobby with dozens of gift baskets on rolling carts.

"Merry Christmas," Sera said with a smile. She looked pretty, wearing a red and white velvet dress with a thick red headband that pulled her dark curly hair away from her face.

My throat went dry, she was so pretty, but somehow I managed to say, "Merry Christmas."

She looked just as elated as I was.

Together, we went through all of the baskets, making sure they were perfect before taking them to the kids. Luckily each basket looked exactly like we'd planned and was wrapped in iridescent cellophane and tied with curled red and white ribbons.

"We'll start in the children's playroom," Sera said, reiterating our plan. "The families will be meeting us there in just about fifteen minutes."

We got to work taking the baskets for the children upstairs on rolling carts. Along the way, we could see hospital staff rolling food carts to patients that held a special Christmas breakfast. The hospital had gone all out. There were pancakes, waffles, bacon, sausages, hot cocoa from Cocoa Corner, and more cookies than I'd ever seen in my life.

My stomach rumbled loudly at the smell, even though all the food was covered with clear plastic.

Sera laughed. "Me, too."

Soon after we had all the baskets lined up around the room, the families began pouring in. Some of them were dressed casually, others in matching Christmas pajamas, and one family was dressed up like they had planned to go to church.

Sera grabbed my hand to lead me over to them. I liked having her hand in mine, although she dropped it too soon.

Once everyone arrived and got settled in, Sera and I took the floor. The parents sat in the chairs at tables all around the room while the kids sat on the carpet patiently but excitedly.

"Good morning," Sera said.

"And Merry Christmas!" I added. "Who's excited to open presents?"

The kids screamed and cheered so loud my ears hurt.

At first, I thought my ears were ringing, but then I realized the sound was music carrying in from the hallway. It got louder and louder as I turned to Sera, who looked just as puzzled.

Then a large group of women filed into the room, singing "We Wish You a Merry Christmas."

"The Carol Karens," Sera exclaimed near my ear so I could hear her. "I didn't ask them to be here. Did you?"

I shook my head. No way I had that kind of pull in Garland. The Carol Karens got booked months ahead of the holidays. How were they here?

Sera touched my hand, and I turned to see where she was looking. Her parents were waving through the glass as they stood in the hallway. Several doctors stood with them, clearly wanting to peek in and see what was going on.

The kids began clapping. Some of the parents began singing along. One of the Carol Karens passed out little jingle bells, and the kids shook them to the song. The whole room felt magical.

I gave Sera's hand a squeeze. She turned to me, kind of surprised. "You did it," I told her.

Tears filled her eyes as she wrapped me in a hug. "*We* did it," she said. "We did it." It felt good to have her hands around my waist. Being able to hold her made the moment even more special.

Once the Carol Karens had fluttered off to

their next gig, the kids sat down on the carpet again. Sera spoke up, saying, "I know this isn't the ideal place to celebrate Christmas. But I hope you know so many people in Garland and around the world pitched in to help you feel loved. Merry Christmas, everyone."

One mom began tearing up, and I handed her a tissue from one of the small tables nearby. Then we began passing out gift baskets, making sure each kid got one of their own.

The kids tore into them, yelling when they saw something they really liked.

The toys, the socks, and candles. There was even a framed picture so they'd always remember this particular Christmas in Garland.

One little boy ran up to me and gave me a big hug. "This is the best Christmas ever!"

After that, the rest of the kids followed suit, hugging Sera and me both. We looked at each other over the little kids' heads, grinning like crazy.

The kids went back to playing, the parents joining them on the carpet.

Sera looked at me and grabbed my hand again. "It really is, isn't it? The best Christmas ever."

"Not quite yet," I told her.

She looked at me, a little confused.

Then I leaned down, held her face in my hands, and kissed her. When I pulled back, I said, "Now it's perfect."

She smiled wide, and I smiled back, knowing I'd never forget this moment.

# 27
## SERA

Since we raised more money than our goal, Paxton and I ordered extra presents so every patient in the hospital could get something for Christmas. By the time we delivered presents to all the patients and ate lunch in the hospital cafeteria, it was the middle of the afternoon. Paxton and I walked out of the hospital into the pale sunlight filtering through the clouds.

"What is that…?" Paxton's voice trailed off.

I looked up and realized Rudolph's sleigh was waiting at the opening to the parking lot. When he saw us coming out, he said, "Paxton, Sera?"

"That's us," Paxton said.

The old man driving the horse-drawn carriage said, "I have a ride for you two."

"Really?" I asked. This was one Christmas activity in Garland that never got old.

He nodded. "Your parents said to tell you Merry Christmas."

Paxton and I looked at each other with a smile. I hadn't realized our parents were in communication, but in a small town like Garland, I shouldn't be surprised.

Paxton gestured toward the carriage. "After you." He offered his hand to help me up, and I happily took it, stepping into the wooden ride. Rudolph had thick woolen blankets waiting for us in the back. I got under one and held it up so Paxton could slide in beside me.

Once he was underneath, he held my hand atop the wool. Even though we were both had winter gloves on, it felt special.

Rudolph called out for the horses to move and soon the iron of their horseshoes plodded against the snow-packed asphalt as they carried us away from the hospital toward the town center.

I looked at the town passing by, incredulous at how life had changed over Christmas break.

I'd gone from feeling invisible and average to being seen by Paxton and having hope for my future.

As we rode by Cider Center and the giant Christmas tree, I remembered my wish.

To be more than just Dr. Lopez's daughter.

It had come true, or rather, it had been true all along. I just needed help to realize it.

"What is it?" Paxton asked. "Everything okay?"

I glanced back at him, smiling. "Everything's more than okay." I gave his hand a squeeze. "It's perfect."


THANK you for reading Curvy and Bright! Want more sweet romance by Kelsie? Visit kelsiebooks.com!

I have wanted to write a snowboarding romance for SO LONG!

My first time snowboarding, I was around twelve years old. I fought with my mom about blowdrying my hair before going out on the mountains and fell on my butt about a million times while I was out there. (But at least my hair was dry, so I didn't get hypothermia. LOL)

Falling and shouting matches aside, I remember how good it felt to stand at the top of a mountain and skim down on a board. It was the closest thing I've felt to flying.

Year after year, I begged to go back, but growing up in Kansas, getting to ski wasn't something we could do or afford all that often. I only rediscovered my love of the sport after college.

That's when I was lucky enough to score a gig writing blogs for Ski New Mexico, which meant I could go snowboard at different ski areas in New Mexico. At first, I was nervous my older, plus size body wouldn't hold up to the slopes like it had as a kid.

But with some lessons and practice, I found myself *flying* again.

At every size and age and skill level, there has been always been a moment when I stop on the side of the mountain with the board strapped to my feet, let my breathing slow, and take in nature around me. It's a sacred moment I haven't experienced anywhere else. I would love for everyone to get that feeling.

I hope this book brought a moment of peace like that to you, whether you live in the mountains or the plains or on a beach (where I would also love to be!). And I hope maybe this story encourages to you try something new like Sera. Even if you're giving it a second (or third) chance.

It's hard to be a beginner, but that feeling of flying is definitely worth the occasional fall.

## ACKNOWLEDGMENTS

I'm so excited this body positive Christmas story is out in the world! I have a few people to thank, so let me make it short and sweet like this story!

My husband and children – you rock (around the Christmas tree! ;))

Team Kelsie – thank you for taking such good care of my readers and me!

Yesenia Vargas – thank you for your help with this story! I couldn't have done it without you!

Jordan Truex – thank you for your expert editing skills! Short novels aren't always easy for me to write, so thank you for making this one better!

Courtney Encheff and Patrick Jean-Jacques – thank you for narrating this story and bringing it to life for my listeners!

Najla at Qamber Designs – thank you for the *gorgeous* cover design!

And you, Sweet reader – you make this Christmas season even merrier. Thank you for reading!

Kelsie Stelting is a body positive romance author who writes love stories with strong characters, deep feelings, and happy endings.

You can often find her writing, spending time with family, and soaking up too much sun wherever she can find it.

**Hang out with Kelsie in her online readers' group!**

**<u>A Curvy Girl Christmas</u>**

Santa Loves Curvy Girls

A Curvy Carol

A Curvy Wonderland

Curvy All the Way

Curvy and Bright

**<u>The Curvy Girl Club</u>**

Curvy Girls Can't Date Quarterbacks

Curvy Girls Can't Date Billionaires

Curvy Girls Can't Date Cowboys

Curvy Girls Can't Date Bad Boys

Curvy Girls Can't Date Best Friends

Curvy Girls Can't Date Bullies

Curvy Girls Can't Dance

Curvy Girls Can't Date Soldiers

Curvy Girls Can't Date Princes

Curvy Girls Can't Date Rock Stars

Curvy Girls Can't Date Surfers

Curvy Girls Can't Date Point Guards

Curvy Girls Can't Date Curvy Girls (Pride Edition)

**The Texas High Series**

Abi and the Boy Next Door

Abi and the Boy Who Lied

Abi and the Boy She Loves

Chasing Skye

Becoming Skye

Loving Skye

Always Anika

**The Pen Pal Romance Series**

Dear Adam

Fabio Vs. the Friend Zone

Sincerely Cinderella

**Standalone YA Romance**

Road Trip with the Enemy

**YA Contemporary Romance Anthologies**

The Art of Taking Chances

Two More Days

**Nonfiction**

Raising the West